MW00415854

Song Stories

Music That Shaped Our Identities and Changed Our Lives

Edited by **Kyle Bylin**

Thank you for everything!

Kyle Bylin

Music: My Religion Press

12141 66TH ST. NE

Adams, ND 58210

ISBN 978-1-48358-604-5 (hardcover)

ISBN 978-1-48358-605-2 (e-book)

"Intro" by Kyle Bylin [Rights Reserved.] "1) Brand New – Logan to Government Center" by Sachi Kobayashi [Rights Reserved.] "2) Victor Shores – Scruffy Nerfherder" by Derek Pinnick [Rights Reserved.] "3) No Doubt – Just a Girl" by Alison McCarthy [Rights Reserved.] "4) Cypress Hill – Illusions" by Matthew Billy [Rights Reserved.] "5) *NSYNC – I Want You Back" by Amanda Krieg Thomas [Rights Reserved.] "6) Genesis – Invisible Touch" by Darren Hemmings [Rights Reserved.] "7) Elliott Smith – Between the Bars" by Cortney Harding [Rights Reserved.] "8) Bob Dylan – Shelter from the Storm" By Sam Chennault [Rights Reserved.] "9) Greg Laswell – I'd Be Lying" by Katie Liestman [Rights Reserved.] "10) Steeleye Span – Long Lankin" by Solveig Whittle [Rights Reserved.] "11) U2 – Sunday Bloody Sunday" by Dane Johnson [Rights Reserved.] "12) The Velvet Underground" — Oh! Sweet Nuthin'" by Marc Ruxin [Rights Reserved.] "13) Metallica – One" by Joey Flores [Rights Reserved.] "14) R.E.M. – Carnival of Sorts (Box Cars)" by Jay Coyle [Rights Reserved.] "15) Jon Hopkins – Light Through The Veins" by Julian Gijsen [Rights Reserved.] "16) Green Day – Good Riddance" by Shelly Hartman [Rights Reserved.] "17) Nick Drake – Cello Song" by Mike King [Rights Reserved.] "18) Muse – Hysteria" by Alex May [Rights Reserved.] "19) Oasis – Don't Look Back in Anger" by Emily White [Rights Reserved.] "20) Peter Gabriel – Don't Give Up" by Michael Cerda [Rights Reserved.] "21) Edward Sharpe and the Magnetic Zeros – Home" by Tony Hymes [Rights Reserved.] "22) Nine Inch Nails – Hurt" by Kyle Bylin [Rights Reserved.] "23) Tori Amos – Scarlet's Walk" by Jackie Otero [Rights Reserved.] "24) Ben Folds – The Luckiest" by Thomas Quillfeldt [Rights Reserved.] "25) Coldplay – Lovers in Japan" by Caitlin Teibloom [Rights Reserved.] "26) Duran Duran – Careless Memories" by Laurie Jakobsen [Rights Reserved.] "27) Peter Bjorn and John – Roll the Credits" by Jackie Yaeger [Rights Reserved.] "28) David Gray – Shine" by Brendan O'Connell [Rights Reserved.] "29) Wilco – Reservations" by Kara Murphy [Rights Reserved.] "30) David Guetta – Baby When The Light" by Bas Grasmayer [Rights Reserved.]

To contact the author, send an email to songstoriesproject@gmail.com

Website: www.songstories.org

Facebook: facebook.com/tellsongstories

Twitter: @tellsongstories

TRACK LIST

PART TWO

MUSIC AND MEMORIES

PART THREE
LOVE AND LOSS

INTRODUCTION

Songs become a part of the story of our lives. Their lyrics linger inside of us. We recall those words, but what we remember isn't what they meant to the person who wrote them. It's what they mean to us. We relate their lyrics back to the events that have happened in our lives. We interject our personal narrative into their songs, and it feels as though they mirror our own memories and emotions.

Some songs make us happy, while others bring sadness. Some songs connect with our present, and others bring us back to the past. They help us recall memories we've forgotten. Some songs are tied to our personal identities and to particular moments in our lives. Playing the song in later years helps us to recall an earlier event as well as the way we felt about it. This is what music does for us. It connects with the story of our lives. It creates meaning. It helps us understand ourselves.

We build a history of music throughout our lives that is unique to us, shaped by our tastes and life experiences. For many of us, it is the closest thing we have to the journal we never wrote or the diary that has long been packed away. The soundtrack of our lives is an ongoing playlist that we add to with each new experience. Each song holds a different significance, one that evolves as we change and grow as individuals. Unlike old journals and diaries, this soundtrack does not collect dust on a nightstand or in the bottom of a box but is stored on a smartphone that we take everywhere and hold tightly in our hands.

The time had come to collect and share these stories to create a people's history of music. What you'll read in this book are personal accounts of how people's lives have been impacted by specific songs. Elliott Smith's "Between the Bars" set Cortney Harding's romantic notions of adulthood, The Velvet Underground's "Oh! Sweet Nuthin'" played one night at a friend's place and changed Marc Ruxin's musical tastes, and Coldplay's "Lovers in Japan" reminds Caitlin Teibloom of a college breakup and who she became through that experience.

This alternate history, composed of shared song stories, will deepen your understanding of music. It'll extend your interpretation of a song beyond what it means to you to how the song has been experienced by another and the meaning it has created in his or her life. Reading each story and playing the song will allow you to hear what music sounds like through ears other than your own.

I hope reading this book will inspire you to share your own song story.

—Kyle Bylin

For a playlist of the songs referenced in
***Song Stories*, visit www.songstories.org.**

PART ONE
YOUTH AND IDENTITY

"When you chose which genre of music to listen to, you also decided who you were."

1

"Logan to Government Center"
BRAND NEW

By **Sachi Kobayashi**

High school was rough for me. Due to misguided choices, failed attempts at overachieving, spells of depression, and overwhelming restlessness, I ended up going to three different schools, all within the same county. I desperately wanted out of high school. I wanted out of my dysfunctional family. I wanted out of my blue-collar state. I was so miserable that I tried to graduate early, collapsed under the course load instead, and ended up at yet another school.

I don't think I could have survived high school if I hadn't found the local DIY music scene, a vibrant mess of kids from northern Delaware that spilled over into parts of Pennsylvania. It was one of the only spaces where it felt safe to be myself: loud, opinionated, strange, and pissed. During the week, we scene kids were spread out among dozens of different schools, separated in little pockets or alone, but Saturday night we'd converge by the hundreds upon a rented hall or basement for a DIY show. The following week, if you passed another kid from the show on the street, you'd give each other a little knowing nod. I went from feeling like a social pariah to being initiated into a secret club. While the anarchist in me resisted joining anything, another part of me secretly hoped that if I tried hard enough, I might be one of the cool kids.

Bands from Toronto to Tampa would play our shows, but the band that lived in hallowed legend was Brand New. If you could claim that you had been at the American Legion hall shows they played in 2000, you had true scene cred. By the time that *Your Favorite Weapon* came out in 2001, I was utterly obsessed with Brand New. I listened to the album on my Sony Discman for hours on end, analyzing the lyrics for new layers of meaning. It felt as if every listen uncovered a new lyrical gem, like a message in a bottle from singer Jesse Lacey, promising survival to kids like me.

My favorite song was "Logan to Government Center." I had fallen in love on first listen (a friend who was close to the band had a demo tape in his car for months before the official release).

What spoke to me most in this song was its theme of being alone; though I was so involved in the scene that I was putting on shows, I still felt very isolated. As a half-Asian girl whose parents both had multiple college degrees, I was almost the polar opposite of the rest of the kids in the scene, which was ruled by white guys from families that saw college as superfluous. Despite the differences, these were my people. No song reflected this tension or emptiness for me like "Logan to Government Center."

Unlike other kids, I wasn't allowed out on school nights, and my parents often didn't have time to drive me to friends' houses. For years, I blamed them for my solitude. If I'm truly honest with myself though, part of me liked it. At heart, I'm an introvert, and as a latchkey kid, I had lovely, wide swathes of time to be alone with my thoughts, listen to music, write in my journal, or draw. Just like the lyrics of the song, I was alone, but not really lonely. When occasionally I wanted company, I had Brand New who clearly understood me, because they had written "Logan to Government Center."

As an adult, I've tried to listen to the many pop punk bands I worshiped as a teen, but a lot of it only holds up with a thick veneer of nostalgia. Still, "Logan to Government Center" rocks me to my core. To this day, it's impossible for me to listen to this song without feeling a tug on my heartstrings. That introvert misfit kid grew up to be a woman who often feels awkwardly different and secretly loves to be alone, notwithstanding the affections of beloved friends, co-workers, and boyfriends who have always seemed more socially savvy. Fifteen years later, I'm still me, still alone, and still somehow content.

2

"Scruffy Nerfherder"
VICTOR SHORES

By **Derek Pinnick**

I'm standing at the bathroom sink, dazed, scrubbing a mysterious mark off the back of my hand. It's black, possibly an "X," or maybe a smiley face. It's tough to tell now. My ears are ringing like a bomb just went off, and I execute a series of controlled falls in the general direction of my bedroom. I've been punched, elbowed, and pressed into a crowd so tight that I could barely move. As I lay down on my bed, all I can think is, "That was awesome."

This is a pretty accurate summary of most of my after-concert experiences. Growing up in sleepy Minot, North Dakota, there were only two music venue choices: see a band in a local bar, or wait until the North Dakota State Fair was in town and slam on your biggest Stetson hat. It may seem like a strange place to become a lifelong music lover, but it was in this wide, empty space that my affinity for music truly began.

Luckily, I wasn't the first person in town to face this challenge. My musical forefathers created musical spaces, beginning with a place called "The Liberty," which burned down just as I was becoming musically conscious. A litany of venues followed, popping up wherever rent was the cheapest and landlords were the most apathetic, with shows in basements of rental houses peppered in for good measure. The buildings would invariably be in some form of disrepair, but that's what the scene called for. We needed something down-and-out, struggling, clinging on for life, just like we were. I have a lot of cheaply-made demos full of songs that remind me of those days, but none instantly transport me in the way that Victor Shores' "Scruffy Nerfherder" does.

When I hear the tilted, staggering opening guitar line, my legs reflexively tense in preparation to begin jumping and hurling myself around in a wild, violent joy; a strange emotion that seems to only exist for the young and defiant. The song makes me want to scream — to punch, hug, and destroy all in the same instant. "Scruffy" is raw. For four minutes and eight seconds, you can hear the emotion of a man. You can hear his fear, anger, and his longing for meaning and love without an ounce of pretense. You hear the honesty that none of us, whether young or old, often have the courage to share.

I still feel this when I hear "Scruffy," but as I get older, I feel new things, too. I'm approaching 30, and I still play these shows. At the time of writing this, my 2-year-old daughter just watched my band play a show in the stripped-out basement of a building. She danced to every song in her adorable, offbeat way. I hope that's good. I hope that means she'll see the value in creative expression and struggle to find spaces to create her art, to find her own "Scruffy." I hope she'll feel alive, like we did — like we still do.

3

"Just a Girl"
NO DOUBT

By **Alison McCarthy**

The year 1996 was awkward, and not just because I was a moody, gangly pre-teen girl who didn't quite fit in, grumbling my way through the sixth grade in the suburbs of Long Island, New York.

It was also an extremely uncomfortable era for pop music. Grunge was breathing its last breath while Madonna was singing show tunes from *Evita*. The East Coast/West Coast hip-hop rivalry was about to turn lethal, and we were still a year or two away from when the Spice Girls, Britney Spears, Christina Aguilera, and *NSYNC would be broadcast on our television screens via "Total Request Live." It's strange to think that there was a time when pop music wasn't incredibly tied to youth culture — especially in our Taylor Swift/Beyoncé/Katy Perry-ruled universe — but in 1996, the pop airwaves were dominated by the adult contemporary sounds of Celine Dion, Melissa Etheridge, Hootie and the Blowfish, Natalie Merchant, and the *Waiting to Exhale* soundtrack.

Still, 1996 had one major highlight for me. It was the same year No Doubt's *Tragic Kingdom* broke onto mainstream radio. The timing couldn't have been more perfect for an awkwardly skinny, freckle-faced, 12-year-old girl obsessed with music, art, and pop culture, who was just starting to ask questions about the larger world.

Like so many other songs that mattered to me during that era, I first heard No Doubt's "Just a Girl" — their first single off *Tragic Kingdom* — while watching MTV past my bedtime. The music video was fun and catchy, but it had a slight punk edge that spoke directly to my teenage feelings. I was fascinated by Gwen Stefani's and her bandmates' sense of style, which combined both Southern California vintage glam and skater culture. Perhaps most importantly, its satirical message about growing up female and the predetermined gender roles available to girls made me feel understood. It was sassy, angry, powerful, and playful all at the same time, and it made some sense out of the frustration and confusion that came with being a girl quickly approaching adolescence.

In pure nineties fashion, I asked my dad to add *Tragic Kingdom* to his next Columbia House music club order for me. It arrived via snail mail a few weeks later, and from that point on, No Doubt was my band and *Tragic Kingdom* was my album.

On the last day of sixth grade, I got to see No Doubt — along with Weezer and the Lunachicks — live with my best friend. It was the first concert I attended without my parents and my first foray into live punk music, as mainstream as it was. My heart skipped when we arrived at Jones Beach Amphitheater. Suddenly, I saw that I wasn't alone in feeling misunderstood, wanting to ask questions, and stepping outside the box. The venue was filled to the brim with 15,000 other kids who looked and felt like me. I knew I had found my people — my fellow suburban teen punk and alternative weirdos — and that these people, along with this music, were going to make everything okay.

I was right. These weirdos, in this alternative, punk, yet still suburban world soon became my best friends. By banding together to embrace our status as outsiders, our desire to ask questions and our love of music — as well as some very questionable fashion choices (ahem, JNCO jeans) — we got each other through the trials and tribulations and highs and lows of the next two decades. Even today, whenever "Just a Girl" comes on, we still sing every word along with Gwen.

4

"Illusions"

CYPRESS HILL

By **Matthew Billy**

It all seems kind of silly looking back. I attended a public school system that was divided into two social camps while growing up in a suburb of New York City: those who listened to alternative rock and those who listened to hip-hop. Your choice of music had ramifications well beyond taste and musical aesthetics; it impacted how you behaved, how you dressed, and who your friends could be. When you chose which genre of music to listen to, you also decided who you were. I was firmly entrenched in the alternative rock crowd and made sure everyone was aware of it. I proudly donned an array of Smashing Pumpkins t-shirts, covered my notebooks in Pearl Jam stickers, and mourned the untimely demise of Kurt Cobain.

Then one summer, something happened. My neighbor Kathy, who was a few years older than I was, acquired the album *Temples of Boom* by a hip-hop group from Los Angeles called Cypress Hill. This was their follow-up to *Black Sunday*, which contained the seminal song "Insane in the Membrane." She purchased the album because of its second single, "Illusions," and played it over and over again.

Hearing the song on repeat acclimated my ears to the flow of a rap, and pretty soon I started to secretly like the song.

The sitar in the introduction was reminiscent of certain Beatles tracks they made after their visit with the Maharishi, the Indian guru. The way the three-note vibraphone riff in the main-groove interplayed with the electric guitar fascinated me. B-Real's flow over the thick kick and snare drums was mesmerizing, and, of course, his lyrics were laden with everything Tipper Gore and Delores Tucker despised about gangster rap — particularly references to cannabis. The song's perfect mixture of artistry and rebelliousness hooked my adolescent self.

At the same time Kathy was bumping "Illusions" across the street, I had also acquired my first part-time job working on an apple farm. A large percentage of my new-found disposable income was earmarked for purchasing records. Like many before me, I found the Faustian bargain the record clubs offered too enticing to resist. Ten records for the price of one felt like a frugal way to spend my income, future obligations be damned (I don't recall if it was BMG or Columbia House I joined, but I'm pretty sure I still owe them money). Nine of the ten albums I chose were rock albums, but the tenth was *Temples of Boom*. Like Kathy, I began to play "Illusions" over and over again.

"Illusions" was a gateway drug similar to the Schedule I narcotic referenced in B-Real's lyrics. I started to listen to more and more rap songs and buy more and more rap albums. Pretty soon I was a full-blown addict, and like many addicts, I tried to keep it a secret. I was fearful that if the truth leaked my carefully crafted teenage persona would be shattered. In my car, a wood-paneled '92 Plymouth Voyager that spewed blue smoke out of the exhaust pipe because it burned oil, the rap albums were always hidden underneath the rock albums so that if someone were to gaze through the passenger-side window, he or she would see Radiohead instead of Cypress Hill. "Illusions" started me down the path to being a closeted hip-hop fan.

I didn't have to hide in the closet for very long. When I went to college, there was no longer a need to maintain appearances. All the rap albums I had secretly acquired while in high school were displayed prominently in a pile on my dorm room desk. *Temples of Boom* was on the top of that pile.

5

"I Want You Back"
*NSYNC

By **Amanda Krieg Thomas**

My best friend in elementary school had a massive crush on Devon Sawa. I mean, who didn't? *Little Giants, Casper, Now and Then . . .* he was on a roll in the early 1990s. My friend "saw him first" though, and called dibs. I was assigned Rider Strong, who played Shawn Hunter on "Boy Meets World," as my crush instead. My fourth-grade self didn't care. Strong was cute enough, but he could have been any of a number of heartthrobs of the day. The real fun was the game of hunting for photos in *Teen Beat* or *Tiger Beat* and acting out scenarios where they were our boyfriends.

I followed a similar pattern when it came to music. Since my parents weren't music nerds, I don't have memories of lectures on the Beatles or Rolling Stones, a certain record always spinning, or recollection of any definitive musical education being passed down. Music was around, and certain songs and artists stuck with me more than others, like The Eagles, Steve Miller Band, and Dire Straits. I embraced the songs I was exposed to — that's as far as my relationship to music went.

Then *NSYNC happened.

I was 13 when I stumbled across their Disney Channel special, "*NSYNC in Concert." I recall warm weather and a distinct feeling of being stopped in my tracks, possibly even in my bathing suit en route to the pool outside. I wasn't even planning on being there long enough to sit on a chair or the couch, opting instead for a small footstool, where I remained, transfixed, until the credits rolled.

I immediately fell in love with every song they performed, but none excited me as much as "I Want You Back." The opening shift from vocal harmony to sassy synth bass line, the combination of sweetness and attitude — it all just grabbed me. These five attractive, yet quirky guys, who could dance, harmonize, and goof around, had me hooked.

This was the summer of 1998 and I had never heard of *NSYNC. No friend had told me to like (or not like) their music. No one called dibs. I discovered them. They were mine.

*NSYNC and "I Want You Back" transformed me into a devoted fan. I bought both the U.S. and European releases of their self-titled debut album. I read the liner notes and learned the words to all the songs. Any attachment to Rider Strong was tossed aside, and instead, I began hoarding *NSYNC posters so aggressively that even my friends got in on the action, cutting out and saving images they came across for my collection. At the peak, every wall of my room was covered. My first "grown up" concert was an *NSYNC performance in Cleveland, Ohio, which I attended with a camp friend. And of course, I hated the Backstreet Boys.

Two years later, the obsession had waned and the posters were gone, but I still dutifully bought *No Strings Attached* and made the pilgrimage to New Jersey for their show at Jones Beach Amphitheater.

It was the first time I had ever gotten to the sophomore album with a band.

In retrospect, I realize that I did *not* discover *NSYNC. The boy band craze of the 1990s was a machine specifically designed to tug the heartstrings and wallets of as many tween girls as possible. And as a member of the music industry, maybe I should be embarrassed about my musical past, having been so caught up in something so superficial. I'm not, though. Far from it. Being a fan of *NSYNC did not make me unique or cool. It did, however, yield a passion and openness that remains at the foundation of my relationship with music today.

Sometimes a song just makes you happy, and you can't explain why.

6

"Invisible Touch"
GENESIS

By **Darren Hemmings**

Music has a powerful way of attaching itself to your memories.

In most cases, when you ask people to mention a song that connects to a specific memory, they'll get a wistful look and name a song they love; whenever they hear this song, it takes them right back to the place and time of that memory.

What is rarely mentioned is the fact that songs you can't stand are capable of doing the same thing. That's the case with me and "Invisible Touch" by Genesis.

The bottom line is that I can't stand that song. Each time I chance upon it on the radio, the music lover in me is possessed with the urge to destroy whatever system that is playing it. How ironic then, that despite disliking the song (to put it mildly), it is actually connected with some of the happiest memories of my life.

Hearing the song takes me back to a family summer holiday I had in the South of France the year it was released in 1986. My dad, opting to save money, had elected to drive to France instead of fly. The only tape in the car was *Invisible Touch*, and my dad *loved* that record. He pretty much played it on repeat — all the way to France, all around France, and all the way back to the UK again.

As a result, in my mind's eye, I get visions of exotic spots like St. Tropez whenever the song comes on. I'm sitting in the back seat of my parents' car, next to my sister. The air is fresh and warm, with the scent varying between clean sea air and jasmine depending on where we were at the time.

It's not that I vehemently hate "Invisible Touch." It's just that when it is one of only eight songs you've heard over and over for two straight weeks, it tattoos itself onto your consciousness whether you want it there or not. Mercifully, my memories of that holiday are all positive and now I remember them with that rose tint of nostalgia that makes me miss those simpler days when my biggest concern was where I could purchase some of those 'dynamite' style fireworks that were illegal in the UK.

Nonetheless, as a song, it remains a strange anomaly to me because hearing it always evokes amazing, warm, loving memories of a perfect childhood holiday. Yet, I can't escape the fact that the song is unbearably twee. I would never elect to play it, but perhaps that is why there's no denying that for all my loathing of the track, I always love that initial moment when I hear it and instantly I am back in the South of France, the sun on my face, not a care in the world, with everything being glorious and perfect.

Since I don't own the song, it pops up like an unexpected surprise at strange, random times in my life — and despite the track making the skin on this music snob itch, the memories that come flooding back are always so very welcome; the song is an immediate tonic for the soul.

7

"Between the Bars"
ELLIOTT SMITH

By **Cortney Harding**

The sensory memory I always associate with "Behind the Bars" by Elliott Smith is of a cool, drizzly night, the sidewalks cleaned by the rain. I'm in an alley between two bars somewhere in Portland, Oregon, probably on NW 21st Street, back up against a wall, while some handsome indie rocker kisses me furiously. I'm drunk and I haven't a care in the world.

That was the image I had of my life when I was 16 years old and Elliott Smith's *Either/Or* was released. Having discovered Elliott Smith via a friend's cool older brother, and after seeing him play in coffee shops, I was fully prepared to love the record. "Between the Bars" stuck out for me because it came out right around the time I started picturing adulthood, and what I wanted adulthood to look like. I was also enamored of the Portland indie scene, dying to be one of the hip kids and not just some juvenile hanger-on. I wanted to be equal to the artists I admired, to be one of them, part of the in-crowd.

My parents rarely drank, and I wasn't much of a drinker as a teenager, but my image of adulthood always revolved around hanging out in bars, having deep conversations, and staying until the last call. When Smith sang about drunkenly making out while looking at the sky, it was quite possibly the most romantic thing I could imagine. I was a weird, precocious (and honestly, pretentious) kid, and I cared little for teen culture, instead watching talky indie films about twenty-something couples and their problems. Nothing was more grown-up than smoking cigarettes and drinking beer at some dirty dive bar.

Although I had barely lived one lifetime, I liked to imagine that I would accumulate baggage and tragic secrets and would then be driven by the need to find someone who could accept that. It was another marker of adulthood — experiences to be shared at cocktail parties or detailed in memoirs, dark stories about sex and drugs. The idea that I would even have a history that I'd want to forget, and that I would find a man who could help me forget it, was the epitome of the future experience I wanted.

"Behind the Bars" sticks with me now, even though I've had many drunken nights with plenty of men and have no desire to ever make out in an alley again. I did all those things, and they were interesting, and now I am done with them, but I miss that romantic ideal. Adult relationships, as it turns out, are about more than drinking and smoking and talking all night — there are things like house mortgages, vet appointments, and vacation plans that must be dealt with — the mundane stuff of life.

Elliott Smith is also the troubadour of my teens and early twenties — he died when I was 23, and I'll still never forget waking up to the news of his death, right as I was realizing the vision laid out in the song. I'd been out the night before and woke up in a bed in a grody punk house that had a pirate radio station in the laundry room.

When I opened my laptop, I saw the news on Livejournal. I cried before shuffling off to my boring office job to spend the day posting lyrics online and commiserating with other fans on Friendster.

He was the patron saint of Portland, a Portland that no longer exists — of specific bars, restaurants, and experiences that are all long gone. I remember watching him walk down the street with two other nineties-era local music stars, Pete Krebs and Sean Croghan, all wearing identical white shirts and cuffed jeans. I thought, "That's it. That's the future." I had that future for a while, and now it's the past, but hearing the song still makes me feel like it's all yet to come.

8 "Shelter from the Storm"
BOB DYLAN

By **Sam Chennault**

I don't remember the first time that I heard Bob Dylan's "Shelter from the Storm." I must have been 12 or 13, living in rural, central Louisiana, having just purchased *Blood on the Tracks*, which I don't remember buying either — though it must have been shortly after I discovered Dylan. For me, this experience had the gravitas of Columbus discovering America. It was the revelation of a seemingly new land for a kid whose friends rocked the Adidas shoes and Kangol hats of Run DMC or worshiped at the spandex-clad, aerosol-scented altar of Def Leppard and Bon Jovi. Rap offered me a hyper-aggressive, masculinized window into urban life, and metal mostly presented me with naked women spread across luxury cars or wrapped around the stripper poles of the Sunset Strip.

Compared to that, "Shelter from the Storm" could only offer a 12-year-old a vague intuition that adult life is a long, sad affair punctuated by brief, clumsy attempts at intimacy and transcendence, but mostly marked by restlessness and failure.

I understood this many years later as I listened to the song while dicking around in western Virginia during my mid-twenties. I was waiting tables, trying to sweat out a nasty pill addiction, and waiting for life to happen, though I was scared that it wouldn't. I listened obsessively as Dylan described feeling exhausted and buried as he moved through a dying world filled with desperate people fighting for warmth and a sense of belonging.

This song, and that burned out feeling, were there in the wee hours of the morning on August 29, 2005. I was living in South Beach, Florida, working as a music journalist and editor for a local paper. Earlier that day, I had been working in downtown Miami, covering the red carpet of the MTV Video Music Awards, with its endless procession of celebrity faces. When I returned home well after midnight, I found out that Hurricane Katrina, which had made landfall in South Florida earlier in the week, was on the cusp of destroying my home state and reverting the swamps and small, already-deserted towns to a place "void of form."

At that time, that metaphor of Dylan's manifested and became literal.

Mostly, the song works in shadows. The shifting tenses and complex structure obscure the narrative, smudging its pain and longing, making it both more diffuse and more universal. When Dylan recorded the track, he had just separated from his longtime wife, the mother of his children, and he was a few years away from being "born again" into evangelical Christianity. You can hear those two poles in how he reaches for the solace of spirituality. In the song, he leers at the girl with silver bracelets on her wrist who takes his crown of thorns, and he ends his travels in a hilltop village, where villagers gamble for his clothes as he contemplates salvation.

I'm not sure I grasped any of this when I was 12, watching the disc rotate in a red blur through the window of my Sony Discman, but listening now, I understand that Dylan is both the subject and object of this redemption. He yearns to be free and to be whole, but he doesn't find these things in a lover's caress or in the things they teach you in a temple. The shelter he describes isn't a physical place or even a spiritual space, but rather, it's in the process itself — the cycles of dissolution, catharsis, and rebirth that we all go through. Sometimes it finds form in the words we write or in the songs we sing, but mostly it's invisible to us.

For most of my life, that would've been a bleak and uncertain prognosis, but over the years, I've found more than a little hope in the song's final stanza where Dylan walks the razor edge of beauty, hoping some day to make it his own.

9

"I'd Be Lying"
GREG LASWELL

By **Katie Liestman**

In 2008, when a good friend of mine posted on Facebook about Greg Laswell's newest album, *Three Flights from Alto Nido,* I knew I had to listen. He didn't gush about artists or albums that weren't top-notch. What I didn't know at the time was that those songs would become the soundtrack to the season my life was in — that post-college, save-the-world, how-do-I-do-this-life one that many go through in their early to mid-twenties. The whole album is a masterpiece, but the song that immediately caught my attention was "I'd Be Lying."

At the time, I belonged to a close-knit community of friends that was serving the suburban metropolis in which we lived. We started a church there, got involved in multiple social justice causes, and did small service projects downtown. We were all misfits in a cookie-cutter town just outside of Houston, Texas called The Woodlands. Somehow we all found each other despite the abundance of trees, three-car garages, and oil companies. Together, we shared a joint purpose, mission, and hope for a better world, and we wanted our town to be the launching pad for us to fulfill this calling.

Post-college life was hard because entering the real world always has its challenges — bills, time management, monotony. On top of that, I was dealing with the loss of a relationship, a death in my family, and the attempted suicide of my brother all within three months. However, even with all of that heaviness, it was also one of the richest, deepest, and most dreamy times of my life. I lived with my best friend, and we hosted many dinner parties, movie nights, and game nights. We also convinced multiple friends to move into our same apartment complex (at one point, 12 of us lived there).

Our evenings were filled with laughter, leftovers, and struggling into adulthood together. Part of that struggle for me included counseling, which I knew I needed, but was hesitant to begin. I never could've survived it without this crew. For anyone who has gone through therapy, you know how exhausting it is. The work is well worth it, but there were many nights I wanted to quit because the process was too daunting. However, I had these friends who pulled me out of my funk into a full life. A few months after I pursued counseling, a handful of my friends set out on the same journey.

"I'd Be Lying" is a narrative of how I saw my little group of friends. While the song is intended to be romantic in nature, I interpreted it in another way. For me, this song is about the connection of community and friendship. Many times, we just need a helping hand to drag us out of the darkness. Or we need to know that someone is there for us, with us, and not going anywhere, even when things get hard.

The trajectory of my life would be completely different if I had not had that crew of people surrounding me at the time. To this day, they are still my "army of fortune," as my husband calls them. Many of them stood with me at my wedding earlier this year, as did I at their weddings. We text often despite being in other cities. We send cards and emails, celebrate together, mourn together, and grow together.

Listening to "I'd Be Lying" is like having an old-school projector of memories flashing through my head of this season. The memories are rich, beautiful, and vivid; I can smell the food we ate, hear the laughter, and feel the love of people who chose me over and over again despite the difficulty. I evangelized this song so much to this group of friends that it was even played at one of our church services and discussed as an example of our calling to community and life together.

I'm pretty sure Laswell would get a kick out of that.

10

"Long Lankin"
STEELEYE SPAN

By **Solveig Whittle**

I spent the summer of my twelfth year in England with my aunt and uncle. Looking back, it was a peculiar sort of thing. My father was British, but he had abruptly left my mother, my sister, and I in America when I was eight. I later learned that he had remarried and settled on the Isle of Wight, his childhood stomping grounds. After his departure, I only saw my father in New Jersey once before he died.

I boarded the British Airways flight to Heathrow as an unaccompanied minor. Uncle David worked in customs, and I remember feeling terribly important because he met me at the door of the plane and whisked me through immigration. Arriving at my aunt and uncle's house outside London, I temporarily fell in love with my 16-year-old cousin Andrew, who had my father's British accent and his very sharp, sarcastic sense of humor. Andrew introduced me to Steeleye Span and to a song on their album *Commoners Crown* called "Long Lankin."

The song is based on an old British folk tale about the murder of the lady of Welton Hall (a real place) and her baby by the character Long Lankin (also known as Lamkin and Lonkin). According to legend, one night when the master of Welton Hall was away on business, the nursemaid, with whom Lankin had made a deal, unlocked a door and admitted the villain. Unable to find any valuables, Lankin roused the lady of the hall and demanded that she tell him where the treasures were hidden. She refused, and in a temper, he killed mother and baby and threw the bodies into a nearby stream. Lankin escaped with whatever he had managed to steal. When the master returned, he set out to find Lankin and exact his revenge. Some say that during the chase, Lankin fell into the stream and was drowned. Others say that Lankin hanged himself in a fit of remorse.

The song tapped into something deeply emotional and perverse about my life that I had no way to articulate verbally. My father's abandonment broke my heart. Because my mother was so fragile emotionally and so angry with him herself, there was no space for me to express my feelings, so I clammed up and pretended my father didn't exist.

I have no idea what went on behind the scenes between my father and his brother that summer, but I never did see my father on that trip to England. I'm certain my uncle and aunt tried to set up a visit to the Isle of Wight, a mere day trip away from their house. Considering I had flown all the way from America, one would think my father could have made time to see me. Perhaps I had been less than enthusiastic to see him when he visited me back in the United States, and he had lost his appetite for rejection. Perhaps he was already in hospital due to the series of heart attacks that eventually killed him at 53. Truthfully, I never asked to see him, which seems rather odd — more than odd — looking back on the circumstances.

I had fun caravanning in France and Switzerland with my cousin, but mostly I remember playing Steeleye Span's "Long Lankin" on the record player back at their house. I came back home at the end of that summer with a new appreciation for melody, harmony, and for the capacity of a lead female vocalist to evoke emotion. I later searched out the vinyl album in college, and later still, bought the CD version. Now, the song can be streamed.

The song still haunts me. It's a ghostly reminder of the restless soul of my younger self, which I still feel walking around inside me sometimes. I know that there are some things I'll never quite get over. Such life experiences, though, have become potent fuel for my creativity.

I continue to use music as a way to express feelings that are not accessible in any other way, to use my lyrics and writing to speak the unspeakable. I've written several songs about friends who have died untimely deaths, although none of my songs are as jolly or macabre as "Long Lankin." My best work is melancholy, bittersweet, and poignant, with a detached vocal that often echoes that of Maddy Prior in "Long Lankin." The lesson I learned from this Steeleye Span song is to make art from the absurd tragedy of life, from the regrets, from the things that can never be re-made or re-imagined because otherwise it would all just be too much.

PART TWO
MUSIC AND MEMORIES

"Great songs take you back to moments you can otherwise not access. To this day, I remember that night and the friendship forged over a love of music."

11

"Sunday Bloody Sunday"
U2

By **Dane Johnson**

I was 12 years old when I first heard the drumbeat driving "Sunday Bloody Sunday," U2's earliest political protest song. All my attention was fixed on the speakers as they were teaching me that poetic angst pairs perfectly with percussion.

I accessed the song through U2's *The Best of 1980-1990* album just before entering my restless high school years. The song would provide me with much-needed identity and rhythm in the seasons ahead. It taught me how to find patterns in complexity, and, ultimately, it made a drummer out of me.

"Sunday Bloody Sunday" begins with drummer Larry Mullen, Jr. cracking sixteenth notes against a snare drum. The hits resound like a slow-motion machine gun. Mullen then stomps in the kick drum with a four-on-the-floor boom, bringing scattered strikes between hi-hat and snare into a pulsing heartbeat. The drums shoulder all of the audience's attention for almost the first 10 seconds of the song.

At the time, these three layers — kick, snare, hi-hat — seemed like clattered chaos, and my untrained mind didn't have time to make sense of its assault on my ears before Bono softened the militaristic rhythm with heartfelt "woahs."

More than wanting to make noise and release pent-up teenage angst, my aspiring musician friends and I longed to express ourselves in a way we couldn't communicate through normal dialogue. We learned quickly that confusion, when cornered, seeks creativity as an escape route. Sometimes, it may leave a trail of art in its wake. I determined that drums and lyrical poetry were the instruments through which I'd be understood.

In spite of listening to the song on repeat for weeks, I couldn't figure out how the three layers went together. My hands, feet, and brain wouldn't cooperate. I signed up for weekly drum lessons and promptly brought the U2's *Best of 1980-1990* CD to my instructor.

He was calm and cool as he listened to the first few seconds of the track. He closed his eyes and bobbed his head. Then, before the song had even reached the chorus, he abruptly turned the music off.

"Ok, let's get crackin'," he said.

What he then taught me was something I've been learning ever since:

"The song might sound complex, but you can always break it down. Once you stop, listen closely, and tackle it one little bit at a time, you'll then be able to find the groove."

Life benefits from the same approach: listen, take it a beat at a time, and settle into a groove. It's funny that a protest song with militant rhythm taught me how to find my peace.

12

"Oh! Sweet Nuthin'"
THE VELVET UNDERGROUND
By **Marc Ruxin**

It happened one brisk evening in the fall of 1988. I was a freshman in college and was midway through an East Coast road trip, having already stopped to see friends at various colleges along the way. When we got to the Rhode Island School of Design in Providence, I remember walking through the city to a divey but incredible Vietnamese place. By the time we stumbled back to my friend Tom's apartment, a dozen beverages into the evening, we collapsed on a pair of threadbare couches next to a few crates of records and an old turntable.

At our small prep school in northeastern Ohio, he and I were among the handful of folks who obsessed over music. He turned me on to the Grateful Dead and Tom Waits, and I turned him on to "alternative music," which at the time included R.E.M., The Smiths, Husker Du, and Cocteau Twins. We would be forever bonded by our shared love of music. Like all true music nerds, we could, and still do, talk about music for hours, arguing about the relative merits of specific songs or albums.

At some point, he dropped the needle on the Velvet Underground's final album *Loaded*. This was a remarkable choice because it not only very appropriately described our state of mind at the time, but for me, it was like finding the missing piece to a puzzle I hadn't realized was incomplete. Immediately, and I mean within the first few notes of the album, my mind was blown and my musical life was changed forever. We must have played the album four times straight without really talking — just lying there letting each precious word and guitar line wash over us.

It was the epic, rambling closing track "Oh! Sweet Nuthin'" that got under my skin, where it has remained for 25 years. In some ways, that song was the bridge between the distant first wave of modern rock bands (that wouldn't occur until a decade after *Loaded* was released) and the music that we now call "classic rock." What the Beatles did for pop music, Dylan for folk, and the Stones for rock and roll, the Velvet Underground did for what would become "independent music." I knew it had to come from somewhere, but I never knew where.

"Oh! Sweet Nuthin'" rides on a smooth, patient guitar line and rock-steady drum line, slowly building into a celebration of the destitute New York characters about whom Lou Reed is singing. The chorus is beautifully echoed by backup singers who lift the song from what would otherwise be a mildly depressing tale to something almost optimistic. It is magic every time I hear it.

Now I understand much more clearly what Lou Reed was going for: it's a song about reinvention, set in the bleakness of a New York frozen in time. I lived there once, too, and loved that same beautiful grit. Like *The Catcher in the Rye*, *Harold and Maude*, and a handful of other exquisite works of modern art that changed my life in

immeasurable ways, "Oh! Sweet Nuthin'" set me on a very different course. I can't imagine who I'd be without it. Great songs take
you back to moments you can otherwise not access. To this day, I
remember that night and the friendship forged over a love of music.

13 "One"
METALLICA
By **Joey Flores**

When I was younger, I lived in a suburb of Sacramento, California. On the other side of the street lived a kid my age who, of course, was my instant best friend. I don't know if it was to save money or because they thought too much TV was bad for my health, but my parents never subscribed to a cable service. Whatever was on regular TV was what we had. Jason, on the other hand, had cable.

It was on Jason's TV that I first saw Metallica's "One" video. It was a 7-minute-and-45-second commentary on the horrors of war, and I was totally entranced by the weight of its message. I had heard the song before, but the video, with its vivid imagery and prolific quotes, made it far more powerful. Though I would ultimately become a passionate follower of politics and an unflinching proponent of peace, this story is not about the impact of the political message in "One." It wasn't until 4 minutes and 35 seconds into the video that my life would change forever, because that's when Lars Ulrich's epic double-bass drum pedal began.

As the camera cut from bombs dropping on muddy soldiers over to Ulrich's feet as he pounded the double bass, I knew in that moment that I wanted to be a drummer. I had never really watched a drummer play like that, nor had I understood how incredible a drummer had to be to play like that. I wanted to be like Lars.

I would spend the better part of my childhood trying to convince my parents to let me play drums, but it wasn't until I was 20 years old that I got my first kit. The irony is that while I never became a great drummer, the influence of "One" may be the biggest of any song in my life.

Ten years ago, while trying to pick drums back up more seriously, I began taking lessons again and met the person who would become one of my best friends, Yotam. Within three months, Yotam and I decided to start a band, though it was him on drums and me as the front man. Through the trying experience of promoting our band, we would ultimately see an opportunity to build an online marketing platform for musicians, and soon after, we founded Earbits Radio.

If not for that fateful day on Jason's couch, I may have never decided to chase my dreams of being a drummer, may never have met Yotam, and most certainly would not have started a company to serve musicians. Nothing has a more profound impact than those things that inspire you to chase your dreams, and for me, that is the power of music.

14

"Carnival of Sorts (Box Cars)"
R.E.M.

By **Jay Coyle**

When I read about R.E.M. for the first time in *Trouser Press* in 1983, I had no idea that they would become one of the bands that defined my life.

Shortly after I first encountered them, I picked up their "Radio Free Europe" single, and, months later, their debut album, *Murmur*. At the time, the album frustrated me; I felt like I was trying to distinguish objects in an out-of-focus photograph. But one weekend near the end of 1983, I saw R.E.M. perform on Nickelodeon's "Livewire" program, and was blown away. Seeing them perform live changed my whole perspective on them.

The second song in the set, "Carnival of Sorts (Box Cars)," hooked me. This song started with the three lead instruments all playing at once. Bill Berry was pounding on his bass drum while also playing on the hi-hats, and since I was a drummer, this pulsing rhythm grabbed my attention. Then, I noticed the chiming sound of the gorgeous black guitar that Peter Buck was playing. Mike Mills was playing a Rickenbacker bass that sounded like a lead instrument on its own. Michael Stipe's lyrics were hard for me to decipher, but none of that mattered when they reached the chorus and the background vocals came in.

I was mesmerized. The band's sound was unique, and yet they looked like normal guys. Unfortunately, the show cut them off before they finished the song. Wanting to hear the end of this great song, I headed out to my local record shop the next week. At the time, I did not know I was searching for their *Chronic Town* EP. Eventually, I found the song on a 12" UK single for "Talk About the Passion" in December 1983.

In the spring of '84, their second album, *Reckoning*, was in my hands and I was quick to buy tickets to see them perform at Rochester Institute of Technology in New York in July of the same year.

Two years later, my obsession with them led me to Georgia, where the group had first formed. It turned out the place held some magic for me, too. Enrolling in the University of Georgia and moving to Athens allowed me to form the two most important relationships in my life.

First, I met my wife, Elaine, in a local bar during our last year in college. It was one of the rare nights when I was not out seeing a band, playing a show with my own band, or drinking, seeing as I was the designated driver for my gang of friends. She passed my music-fan test instantly as we chatted about music, and I invited her to my band's next show.

Being in Athens also allowed me to meet James Williamson, the first friend I made on the UGA campus — all thanks to a pink R.E.M. "Little America Tour" shirt he wore. James and I became fast and dear friends during our freshman year while taking road trips out of Athens to see R.E.M. play shows around the Southeast. After graduation, it was comforting to have him nearby when I moved to Atlanta to be closer to Elaine.

Thirteen years later, James was there for emotional support and helped Elaine and I through the loss of our son, Owen, while also bringing me to faith. Our deep musical connection expanded as he shared a few verses of scripture to offer me guidance and then invited me to his church. This was so impactful at a time when my heart, head, and soul were dark and cloudy having gone through such a jarring loss.

Athens is still a place I have the pleasure to return to for business and I still feel its magic when I am back there. To this day, when I hear "Carnival of Sorts (Box Cars)," I'm instantly transported to the first time I heard the song on TV. Only one poster hangs on my office wall. It has a screenshot of that song's performance as a reminder of the exact moment I fell in love with this song and of what the band means to me.

15 "Light Through the Veins"
JON HOPKINS

By **Julian Gijsen**

I want to take you back three years ago. It's the beginning of 2012 and I've just discovered a little Facebook music group called "Spacebook." Its members are people who like to explore experimental electronic music. They are, for instance, big fans of James Holden, Luke Abbott, and similar artists. I'm amazed at what they are listening to; it seems to have no genre and is so interesting and weird. I literally listen to every track being shared there and while I don't like everything I'm hearing, I'm certainly enjoying the overall experience.

For me, joining this group was a transformative experience. The music truly moved me, inspired me, and allowed me to enjoy life more. Spacebook got me to ditch the kind of cheapish deep house I was playing and lured me to clubs like (the now closed) Trouw, which pulled me even deeper into great electronic music. Spacebook also ignited my search for co-founders of my music website, kollekt.fm. Without it, I might never have found them, missing what has been the best experience of my life. It's my proof that the butterfly effect really exists; we never know the outcome of seemingly small actions.

The track that pulled me into all of this is "Light Through the Veins" by UK producer Jon Hopkins. Some may recognize the song from "Life in Technicolor" by Coldplay, and that's because Hopkins produced that track for them (and has produced many other Coldplay songs). To me, it symbolizes life from beginning to end — with all the emotions connected to it. Life can throw so much at us, but in the end, we need to remember that we're incredibly lucky to be alive and to feel. If we manage to do that, everything becomes much more enjoyable.

This track allows me to dream, smile, and cry at the same time. It makes me feel alive. The synths move together organically, like a seed transforming into a plant, then evolving into a beautiful tree — all in an instant. Then, when everything fades, a heavenly melody emerges to assure me that everything will be all right in the end. This is a song that expresses the greatest happiness as well as infinite hope. I could imagine it being played at weddings as well as at funerals, as it seems to encompass the human condition.

I had never heard of Hopkins' work before, but I have become a big fan. Hopkins to me has the ideal artist profile: humble and pure in his appearance, brilliant in his diverse productions. Oh, and he can kill the dance floor with his live sets, too.

16

"Good Riddance (Time of Your Life)"

GREEN DAY

By **Shelly Hartman**

In 1993, I was stumbling my way through college at the University of Missouri-Columbia as an undeclared major. Having already tried to convince my parents that it actually was a great idea to let me be a theater major and subsequently a film student, I'd pretty much failed at all attempts, having no earthly idea of what I wanted to do with my life.

That month, the issue of *Rolling Stone* with Natalie Merchant of 10,000 Maniacs on the cover arrived in the mail, and a sub-headline caught my eye. It read, "Hit Patrol: How to Work in the Music Business." As I scanned the article, it was as though I could see my future unfolding before me. I realized music had been my passion all along, having played drums for years in school. Since I wasn't good enough to be a musician, I had considered that dream to be dead. It had never occurred to me that I could work in the "business" side of music.

The next day, I scoured the help wanted ads in the student center and found a job listing for an unpaid internship. A month later, I was a proud Midwestern marketing rep for Restless Records, home to such legendary artists as The Replacements, Soul Asylum, They Might Be Giants, T.S.O.L., The Cramps, Ween, The Jayhawks, and The Dead Milkmen. My job was to flood the region's record stores with posters, stickers, and giveaways; pester college radio stations for airplay; get CD reviews in the student paper; and more. I loved every minute of it. I enjoyed hanging out with the artists, calling and talking to DJs, making retail displays with posters, and doing giveaways.

Several years later, I was 24, fresh out of college and working as a receptionist for a modern rock radio station, 98.3 The Buzz FM in Columbia, Missouri. I knew that I needed to move to New York, Los Angeles, or Nashville if I ever wanted to make it in the music business. I chose California because of the ocean, but my father thought moving to LA sight unseen was the worst idea he'd ever heard. I made up my mind to leave anyway and saved all summer to put a measly $1,500 in my pocket.

On my last day at the station, our music director, Paul Maloney, brought me into the booth and asked me to stay for the next on-air segment. To my surprise, he flipped the ON switch and made a point of telling our listening audience how much I meant to the station and the staff and just how many things I did behind the scenes for the station's events and our listeners. Then he dedicated a song to me, Green Day's "Good Riddance (Time of Your Life)." I had never really thought much about the song, but in that moment, the words clicked and fit with my experience.

For me, the radio station was like family. In leaving it, I would be giving up not only the comfort of a job I had loved but also the friends that I had made. I recalled the fun we'd had, throwing televisions, lawn ornaments, and blow-up sheep filled with Jell-O off the top of our radio tower to celebrate Cinco de Mayo one year. Another time, we'd hosted a summer concert festival. I'd made friends who taught me how to do voice-overs and make commercials for local businesses. I'd cleaned the toilets at the station, and I remembered giving away 20 free surprise tickets to Phish fangirls trading bracelets for tickets in the stadium parking lot. I'd also taken all the calls for the music director when he didn't want to hear label reps pitching their songs in hopes of being added to the rotation that week.

Paul brought me to tears by making me think about leaving my "home" and the safety of a job for the unknowns of Hollywood. I drove across the country in a 17-foot U-Haul truck with a broken cassette deck; therefore, radio was my only friend. Green Day's "Good Riddance (Time of Your Life)" was playing in heavy rotation, which meant that I heard that song and cried about three times per hour all the way across the country, knowing I made the right decision, but simultaneously excited and scared.

Now, twenty-plus years later, five corporate layoffs, and eight jobs later, I'm still here, and I'm still kicking. I've had the time of my life, and I couldn't imagine it any other way.

17 "Cello Song"
NICK DRAKE
By **Mike King**

My first gig out of college was working at State Street Bank in Quincy, Massachusetts as a mutual fund accountant. I was a history and politics major in school, listened to a ton of music, and hadn't taken a math course since high school. The details are murky, but I remember some anxiety before graduation about post-college life, a quick meeting with the career advising center at Assumption College, and the assurance that State Street Bank was a great company to work for. I started in June of 1996.

State Street Bank likely *is* a great company to work for, but I found the task of calculating the net asset value for mutual funds on a nightly basis to be extremely difficult and not a great fit for my skillset. Not only was I trying to learn basic accounting in the early mornings before work (I didn't fully comprehend the difference between a debit and a credit, for example), but I also was teaching myself to use the numerical keypad (I had never even heard the phrase "ten key"). In a room full of accounting majors, I was falling behind quickly. I left after four months or so. It was a character-building experience.

Around this time, a good friend of mine, Jon O' Toole, had started an internship at a record label in Salem, Massachusetts called Rykodisc. The work he was doing at Ryko was like a dream, and as far from ten key and net asset value as you could get. Jon got me an interview with the college radio promotions director, and I was offered the position of "unpaid college radio intern." In order to bring in some income, I leveraged my weak financial background to get a part-time job at Scudder Mutual Funds. I would work at Scudder in the morning, change out of my suit in the bathroom at noon, and drive from Norwell, Massachusetts up to Ryko in Salem to work from 1:00-7:00 PM.

While I was familiar with Rykodisc as the label that put out Frank Zappa, Morphine, and Medeski, Martin, and Wood records, I had no idea about the depth of their catalog. On one of my first days in the office, my boss, Jamie Canfield, took me into the mailroom and gave me a 20-minute overview of Ryko's catalog — Ali Farke Toure, Old and in the Way, David Bowie, Elvis Costello, Tom Verlaine — loading me up with key titles from each artist. In particular, I remember very clearly Jamie handing me the first title in Nick Drake's short catalog, *Five Leaves Left*. I was told something along the lines of "put this one on if you want to get the ladies."

On my drive home that night, I listened to what Jamie had given me. While most of the music was amazing (Ryko had some great A&R), the artist that really struck me was Drake. He was like a musical alien — his odd tunings and sparse instrumentation ("Pink Moon," in particular) really appealed to me. I was apprehensive about my move to Ryko and unsure about my future in music, but when I heard "Cello Song," I felt that everything would be okay. How could it not be, when I was working with something so beautiful?

I was shocked to learn a few weeks later that the sales of Drake's entire catalog, according to Nielsen's SoundScan, were only about 90 units a week! Although R.E.M. and The Cure cited Drake as a major influence, Drake's music was still relatively unknown. It became my mission to tell as many folks as possible about Drake. Although one can argue that Volkswagen did the heavy lifting of raising his visibility by using the song "Pink Moon" in a Cabrio commercial in 2000, I like to think I played a small part. Nick Drake and, in particular, "Cello Song" represent the beginning of my professional life in music.

18

"Hysteria"
MUSE

By **Alex May**

Muse has been my favorite band for many years now, due in no small part to its combination of heavy riffs, spacey-sounding effects, and percussive driving force. I'd heard a few of their songs when I was first getting into music, but the song that took them from being *one* of my favorite bands to my *favorite* band was "Hysteria." Upon later seeing this song performed in a recorded live performance, my music hobby instantly evolved into a career goal.

"Hysteria," from Muse's third album *Absolution,* is a song about agitation, impatience, and fruitlessly chasing something you desire. This theme resonated with me, both personally and professionally, as I was chasing a career in music. The song begins with a heavily distorted bass line, which is shortly joined by a rising guitar swell and heavy drum groove. This motif repeats for the majority of the song, punctuated only by an emotional guitar solo and a thunderous breakdown to end the song. This overall intensity reflects the frustrated but somehow hopeful mood that seems to accompany my pursuits.

Listening to "Hysteria," I picture the band's performance during Glastonbury's 2004 headline show — arguably the gig that brought Muse into the wider public's attention. On a family vacation in June of 2006, I purchased the deluxe edition of their newly released *Black Holes & Revelations* album, which came with a live video recording of the aforementioned gig. On the road trip to our destination, I popped the disc into the portable in-car DVD player that my sister and I shared and began to watch the performance on a screen that wasn't much more than nine inches wide. Despite the small size, I became completely engulfed.

I vividly remember sitting in our family's dark blue Honda Odyssey, watching the band open the show with "Hysteria," and being blown away by the sheer scale of the performance. I had been to concerts before, but Glastonbury's crowd of 150,000 easily trumped their audiences. Not even through the first song yet, I saw that what could be done with music was far beyond what I imagined. The scale of the crowd and the encompassing style now fuels my own music taste, lofty goals, and ambitions.

I've been somewhat of a visual listener for as long as I can remember, and the music I hear creates vibrant images in my mind. I'm drawn to music that gives me joy or comfort. With "Hysteria," I picture a neon-lit English skyline, large crowds of passionate people, and instruments that evoke strong moods. "Hysteria" sparked my interest in British music and culture, and it still has the power to create the type of mental picture that I seek in other kinds of music.

My fascination with Muse has grown exponentially over the years as my learning about music composition and production increases. "Hysteria" represents what I hope to achieve, despite all of the obstacles along the way. This song perfectly captures the pursuit of personal fulfillment, and the song's album artwork that I have tattooed on my left arm is a daily reminder of this. Listening to "Hysteria" is a hopeful motivator that shows me what just a few people in a band can achieve through music.

19

"Don't Look Back in Anger"
OASIS

By **Emily White**

When I was 13 years old, my neighborhood girlfriend and I used to watch MTV every morning until we had to walk to school. For whatever reason, the channel seemed to play Oasis at 7:25 AM every morning, right before we had to leave the house. I have vivid memories of the video being played at this time — it was "Don't Look Back in Anger."

Now, at 32, when I saw that Noel Gallagher — who penned and sings the song — was playing at my favorite venue in the world, The Pabst Theater in Milwaukee, I knew I had to be there with my middle school friends. When I went to buy tickets to the show, I was stunned to find out that it was not sold out! I believe it sold out eventually, but to me, a living legend was gracing Wisconsin with his presence, and we should all be so grateful.

Once the show began, the audience became a family — of Brits, of Milwaukeeans, of fans from Japan who were attending every show on the global tour. Noel ended the show with the song that generates such profound memories of time spent with my girlfriends in 8th grade, the song that took on the same meaning 20 years later as I saw it being performed with people that I still — and will always — feel a deep-rooted connection with.

Noel's lyrics are generally quite simple. After all, he has often said that writing lyrics is not the part of songwriting he feels he is best at. Yet the idea of getting out of his tough part of town, his broken home, and his abusive childhood resonates on a unified front as many of us wish of faraway places as teenagers.

I didn't grow up in a tough part of town or in a broken and abusive home, but I certainly wanted to start a revolution from my bed. I wanted to get out of my town, to never stop seeking or creating, and to never look back. Or at least to look back on my life in a peaceful manner.

Noel Gallagher is possibly rock's last great rock star, at least in the classic rock realm. He is the musical son of the '60s and his music is admittedly derivative. At his shows now, I see sons and fathers who are trying to pass the music on, and who knows how long that will last as genres continue to evolve and change.

One of my favorite things about traveling the world is that pop music can be a grounding and uniting force no matter where you are. I have heard "Don't Look Back in Anger" played in many settings throughout the years, from airports to restaurants abroad. Yet the simple melody and lyrics will always bring me back to my friends in middle school and the importance that Noel's music and this song played in our lives. The simple yet powerful lyrics are strikingly memorable on multiple levels. Which was extra powerful considering Oasis was and still is my favorite modern band. The Beatles are ultimately my favorite artist ever, yet amazingly I still don't hear the musical comparison between the two, despite Noel admitting that he stole songwriting elements from his beloved ultimate band.

People always say, "Don't meet your heroes." I feel forever fortunate for that statement to be wrong in my case. When I did finally meet Noel, over a decade after his music influenced me to pursue a career in the music industry, he was incredibly kind. He was so kind that after his set, he said, "Did you hear me dedicate 'Don't Look Back in Anger' to you?" I actually didn't, as I had been enjoying the show at the side of the stage with friends at that time despite the muddy side-stage sound. But luckily, with the magic of the YouTube, I can rekindle the memories of the power of this song as well as the songwriter's kindness at a moment's notice.

I will forever look back on my youth, my career in music, my friendships, and my life experiences with peace thanks to this song. It's meaning ties together memories of Noel's storied childhood intertwined with my own memories as a young person. I always have Noel to remind me not to look back in anger, no matter the circumstances.

20 "Don't Give Up"
PETER GABRIEL
By **Michael Cerda**

It's 2016. I have an incredible life, with great family, friends, and passions. But it doesn't come for free. It has its trials and tribulations, the good, the bad, and the ugly. My go-to song in a time of need has been private until now, but it's a recurring one: "Don't Give Up" by Peter Gabriel. I was singing along with it in my car on a commute just a few weeks ago for the hundredth time.

In college, I was playing in a band, selling out regional venues, touring up and down California, and looking at record deals. I was also seeing an amazing girl I had been fond of since high school, and somehow, she became pregnant. No, it wasn't an immaculate conception, but it changed everything.

The situation felt like life prompting me to embrace it. Life has a way of doing that. It's easy to fall victim to circumstances, but it's usually best to rise to any challenge and make those circumstances a part of who you are. For me, embracing the situation was an opportunity to get my act together and think beyond college to the future, possibly beyond chasing record deals.

In August 1994, our daughter was born, and I still had about five months of school left. I earned money playing my music and working as an assistant manager at KFC. Periodically, I would barter the leftover chicken with a local Domino's Pizza, just so that we weren't eating 3-piece chicken dinners every night. Needless to say, I cut off my long hair, bought an interview suit, and began the journey to an adult life with my new family.

I interviewed long and hard. My major was industrial technology, so it was a little bit of everything in the business/technology process. I talked to a urinal company in Paso Robles, CA, a chipset company in Chandler, AZ, a personal finance company in Long Beach, CA, a trucking company in Adelanto, CA, a computer systems company in Wheeler, IL, and a graphic arts scanner company in Oakland, CA. As I drove around trying to find a job that would support my new family, all sorts of questions came to mind: Am I going to make it? Are we going to get married? Can I actually support my family? Will I ever play music again? What if none of this works?

More than 20 years later, I still vividly remember driving down Highway 5 on my way to these interviews, wondering whether I could find a job that would be profitable and meaningful. I remember listening to a live version of Peter Gabriel's "Don't Give Up," the version from the "Secret World" tour, which featured Paula Cole on vocals. She sang the Kate Bush parts. Those were particularly special. The stern verses contrasted with the uplifting chorus, and the outro was an all out groove session. Tony Levin's bass drove the song from start to finish. But the Paula and Kate vocals about not giving up and falling back on your family were what got to me, and still do.

As I write this essay, I listen to this song, and it still brings a tear to my eye. After all, for me, it represents the present, the past, and the future. It's like a time capsule that envelops you in every possible context or event in your life. From every moment of your past and in every future event, that song will be there. There's something profound about that. Nobody talks about this kind of thing, but I know people think it.

Slowly but surely, things began to work out. She said yes. I finished school. We married with our own daughter and my sister as the flower girls. Life got moving. But the faster it moved, the more challenges appeared.

All throughout, I kept that Peter Gabriel tape handy. When I got a car that had a CD player, I kept the CD in the glove box. It's still my go-to song. My current car doesn't have a CD player, though, so now I look up the song on my phone, press play, and sing along.

PART THREE
LOVE AND LOSS

"As life moves on songs move with us, transporting us back to different moments and experiences. Feelings come rushing back, and the memory of those feelings come bubbling to the surface."

21

"Home"

EDWARD SHARPE AND THE MAGNETIC ZEROS

By **Tony Hymes**

I've never been to Alabama. I've never been to Arkansas either, but as soon as I hear those two words, sung so beautifully in the duet "Home," I'm overwhelmed by a feeling of love. Even at the very beginning of the song, with the first few notes of an unforgettable whistled melody, I'm immediately transported through memories of my wife and our entire journey together.

She had visited a nauseating 14 apartments before she stepped into mine as a 23-year-old French girl who had dodged rats, climbed down slimy metal staircases, and choked on the vapors of the Chinatown fish market all in search of a place to live in New York City for a two-year work contract. A smile grew across her face when she walked in: the warm lighting, the exposed brick, the split-level style. No odd fish smell. And me. She didn't know for sure yet, but she had found her new home.

I know what it's like to move around the world and not know anybody, having done it a few times already in Italy and Spain. I took Magali under my wing, and we did everything together: brunches at Flea Market, dancing at The Woods, drunken cab rides over the

Brooklyn Bridge with the cold lights of the city blurring into inter-woven streaks of warmth stretching across the East River. It wasn't long before love sparked, and when we stood atop Belvedere Castle in Central Park, she turned to me and told me she was so excited she couldn't feel her hands. It might have just been the cold. I took them and kissed her.

A few months later, we held our first rooftop party, the one that began two summers of BBQs, burgers, watermelon kegs, and dance marathons. At that first party, just as the sun was setting and orange reigned in the New York sky, "Home" came on our Pandora station. Magali jumped up and took my arms and we danced in circles across the silhouetted skyline of lower Manhattan. From that moment on, when-ever she heard that song, she would tell me: "Home is here with you."

Her visa was up 18 months later, and she wanted to go back to France to continue her career. I had two options: potentially lose this love or drop everything and go with her to a country where I didn't speak the language and had only visited a few times. There was no real decision. I was going to follow her to Paris and leave my home again.

I slept for almost two weeks straight when we arrived, so heavy was the come-down from the intense energy of New York City. I was introduced to my new social circle of Magali's friends and fam-ily. I struggled through the difference between *le* and *la* and *un* and *une*. For money, I fixed up and painted apartments, sanding plaster until my lungs choked. One thing pushed me through — that song. Whenever we would hear it, no matter how difficult something had been, a smile arrived, and I told Magali, "Home is here with you."

When we got married, it was clear that our lives would always be spent in some sort of travel, whether she was far from her home, me far from mine, or the two of us off in some other corner of the globe. "Home" means more to me than every other song put together, because it makes our adventurous life possible. I engraved the lyric from the chorus on the inside of my wedding ring.

We danced until the sun glistened in the morning dew at our wedding in the French countryside, at the same place that JFK spent his state visits back in the 1960s. Over 50 Americans came, matched by over 100 French, and under wrought-iron chandeliers and ivy that trickled down in green rivers, we celebrated our international union with our song. Thereafter fixed in our friends' and families' minds, they inevitably play "Home" whenever we visit anyone.

Now Paris has become my home, and we've carved out a place here that I could have never imagined when we stood in apartment 6B on East 13th Street with our last bags en route to the airport, crying uncontrollably. Through my wife, I found many opportunities, like meeting the guys that I would spend three years working with at Whyd, a social music network. Her family here has become mine too, along with a commendable troupe of buddies and friends.

We finally saw Edward Sharpe and the Magnetic Zeros at the mythic Olympia here in Paris last winter. Needless to say, I was turned into a human-sized goose bump when the whistling started at the beginning of the song, and as the band members danced across the stage and we danced across the audience, I took my wife's arms and was transported back to the rooftop where we danced to all the possibilities that the world could give us as long as we're "home."

22

"Hurt"
NINE INCH NAILS

By **Kyle Bylin**

For the past two years, every song I've heard has reminded me of the same person. I can't remember to buy a gallon of milk, but I never forget about my ex-girlfriend. I can summon her ghost with almost any song and haunt myself with her image. I'll be listening to music and washing a dish in the kitchen sink, and in my mind, I'll be holding her around her waist and watching the waves roll across the ocean.

Sometimes, I only revisit this memory for half a second before it fades into the back of my mind. Other times, I move the sponge in a circle and stare into oblivion for so long that I lose track of what I'm doing. For a moment, I'm sitting on the coastline of California and feeling a cool breeze blow her hair into my face. Then, I'm back in my kitchen, looking through a window at a white garage door and reaching to position the plate between the grooves in the drying rack.

The movie theater in my mind keeps replaying these scenes with my ex — they are the happiest and saddest moments of my life. I've watched them a thousand times, and I'll probably see them many more.

When I hear "Hurt" by Nine Inch Nails, the movie rewinds itself to a familiar scene. I'm lying on my bed and looking at the ceiling. I'm imagining my ex backpacking through Europe and worrying that she might get hurt. My body begins to tremble, and tears pour down my face. I'm paralyzed by the realization that I can't protect her. I've lost my sweetest friend. She went away in the end. Nothing else mattered.

I don't know why I chose to listen to that song after a painful breakup on purpose, but I used Trent Reznor's words as a scalpel to cut out my broken heart.

Here's the hardest part about being a sensitive and creative person: I never know who or what is going to hurt me, but I do know exactly how to burn myself. Music is the gasoline that I pour into my ear canals and let flow through my veins until it finds a spark and ignites a flame. I try to figure out how the fire makes me feel and use words to capture the pain that resides within. Music is the light that illuminates the dark — it helps me see the emotions I feel.

As I listen to "Hurt" and write this essay, I realize that I didn't know what an empire of dirt looked like until the second the tiny grains of soil slipped through my hands. My fistful of money and power twisted like a tornado as it fell back down to earth. It reunited with all of the dead people that it never made happy.

Nowadays, I don't want to sit on the California coastline anymore. I wish the film projector would break and the movie theater would close. I chased my dreams to Los Angeles and got in over my head. I fell in love with a Minnesota girl because she reminded me of home, and soon enough, North Dakota is where I returned.

"Hurt" helps me remember someone that I'll never forget.

23

"Scarlet's Walk"
TORI AMOS

By **Jackie Otero**

I've found that the most well-crafted songs have three layers of meaning: literal, intended, and interpreted. The literal meaning is universally understood from the first time you hear a song, while the intended meaning is an intimate secret only known to the songwriter and can be debated and picked apart to a fan's delight. However, the interpreted meaning is the one that strikes each person differently; it is a personal reflection unique to each listener and often unknown to the artist. In the early 90s, I was introduced to an artist whose songs were rich with all three types of meaning: Tori Amos. Seen by outsiders as a fairy-loving cuckoo, she was known to her diehard fans (me among them) as a soul-baring goddess.

As I grew out of my most angst-ridden teenage years, Tori's songwriting matured, shifting from lyrics about love and rejection to stories about America, motherhood, and history. The album *Scarlet's Walk* was released in late 2002, past the peak of her alternative commercial success, and the title track was far from a standout, lacking a catchy hook or signature flirtatious snarl. However, its release

LOVE AND LOSS

coincided with a difficult period in my life, and my interpretation of the song still brings tears to my eyes every time I hear it.

The song begins and ends with a haunting chant. Through this framing device, Tori indicates that the song is part of her sonic tale about Native Americans being ousted from their land. Her great-great-grandmother was a Cherokee who survived the Trail of Tears, and this is a personal account of a dark period of ethnic cleansing. Literally, Scarlet is the female protagonist of the album; she takes a journey through America, digging into corners of our country's past. Perhaps Scarlet is meant to represent Tori herself, or a collection of women in Tori's life, but I found a place in my own life for Scarlet.

My grandmother was born in 1918, and her world was colored by her formative years in the Depression. She taught us how to use every bit of toothpaste in the tube by using a razor to slice it open. She told us stories about my grandfather's service in World War II on the ill-fated PT-109 and her bond to my grandfather's skipper, who later became the 35th President of the United States, John F. Kennedy. She could travel back in an instant to decades earlier, even though she forgot our names when she saw us by the fall of 2002, just weeks after the release of *Scarlet's Walk*.

After my grandmother experienced a frightening fall, my family made the tough decision to move her out of the small home where she had lived independently for several decades, raising her eight children and living her later years as a single woman active in the senior social scene. Her new home became a rehabilitation and hospice center on Scarlet Road in our hometown of Orlando, Florida.

My mother and I played the song over and over on trips to visit my grandmother during the last few months of her life. Tori reassured us that my grandmother was free to leave the earth without carrying the emotional debts of her past struggles. It was her path to follow, and she could go in peace.

"Scarlet's Walk" became my grandmother's final steps toward her resting place, and it allowed us to accept the release of her body from the earth, our terra. Today, I drive by Scarlet Road each time I make my daily commute, and I think of my grandmother's final days, her positive impact on the lives of my huge extended family, and the song that helped us grieve and let go.

24 "The Luckiest"
BEN FOLDS FIVE
By **Thomas Quillfeldt**

I've been a massive fan of Ben Folds Five since I stole my brother's cassette of *Whatever and Ever Amen* circa 1999, but I was never that keen on a couple of Folds' solo records. For years, my favourite songs were always the most poignant (some might say maudlin) like "Cigarette" and "Jesusland." Being a Brit, liking Ben Folds' music always felt like a guilty pleasure because it's so very American — saccharine and sentimental.

Early in 2014, I booked a single ticket to see him play later that year in London with the Heritage Orchestra. I had largely forgotten about the show when it rolled around as it was a really stressful time: I was due to get married the same month, work wasn't going well, and I was having some persistent health issues that were making me feel extremely worn out. Spending an evening in the city in your own company when you're suffering from nervous exhaustion leads inexorably to rumination and morose introspection.

On that night at the Barbican — a comfortable, high-end, classical venue — Folds played some favourites, some deep cuts, and a peculiar classical/pops concerto that formed the centerpiece of the first set. The second set passed pleasantly enough and he went off-stage to rapturous applause to prepare for the obligatory encore.

I glanced at the time and felt that pang of tiredness you often experience toward the end of gigs (even if you're enjoying them).

As he began the encore, I realised that I didn't know the tune. The first line of the lyrics spoke to me immediately: *"I don't get many things right the first time / In fact, I am told that a lot."* The next line pulled me in closer: *"Now I know all the wrong turns, the stumbles and falls / Brought me here."* This cut through me like a knife — feeling worn down and attending the show alone, I'd been increasingly feeling self-piteous about my general situation as the night wore on. This plaintive, direct song — new to my ears — resonated with me so strongly that it had me on the edge of my seat.

And then like the schmaltzy cheese ball he is, Folds (figuratively) reached right into my chest: *"And where was I before the day / That I first saw your lovely face? / Now I see it every day."* This line about a long-term loved one gave me a gigantic lump in my throat. In 20 days' time, I was to marry my childhood sweetheart. The first chorus broke me:

"And I know / That I am..."

Feeling pretty choked up Ben, you bastard.

"...I am..."

You don't have to repeat yourself.

"...I am..."

Yes, I know you are, but what am I?

"The luckiest."

And then the tears came — yes, reserved Brits can cry too.

The balladeer proceeded to tear me into little bits with the second and third verses, evoking the bittersweet romance of films like *Eternal Sunshine of the Spotless Mind* and *Cinema Paradiso*: *"What if I'd been born fifty years before you / In a house on a street where you lived? / Maybe I'd be outside as you passed on your bike / Would I know?"* The thought of never having met my wife-to-be kept me blubbering.

At one point it felt as if Folds was pulling thoughts directly from my head: *"I love you more than I have ever found a way to say to you."*

Then, accessing that emotion we all know from the famous opening montage to the film *Up*, he conjured the image of the old couple that feel lost without one another: *"Next door there's an old man who lived to his nineties / And one day passed away in his sleep / And his wife; she stayed for a couple of days / And passed away."*

For me, certain live music shows, particularly classical concerts, are extremely meditative. Your mind has time to wander and loop, to refresh and reflect. By the final chorus though, I was utterly drained, with my thoughts and emotions in a puddle on the floor. This song, this sentiment, at this moment, was exactly what I needed to hear — it struck me like a brick to the temple.

Then the final chorus:

"That I know..."

Crying in public is not very dignified of me.

"...that I am..."

Not holding it together very well.

"...I am..."

A car crash, a train wreck...

"...the luckiest."

Indeed.

25

"Lovers in Japan"
COLDPLAY

By **Caitlin Teibloom**

I'm stuck at a traffic light. My mind, like my iPod, is on shuffle — *did I lock the door to the apartment? Is all the food out of reach of the dog? Is work going to suck today? What the hell am I doing with my life, again?*

As I start moving down the road again, I snap to. There's a familiar piano strain lilting from the car's speakers, and it grabs my attention right away, like seeing a ghost of a past life from across the room. Coldplay's "Lovers in Japan" grabs hold of my psyche, and suddenly, I'm in a small German university town called Freiburg.

You wouldn't think I'd wanted to study abroad at all if you'd seen me the day I left American soil — I was sobbing uncontrollably, scared about flying by myself, about living abroad by myself. I was scared about leaving my serious college boyfriend, Scott, behind, and unsure of what the future would hold for me and for us.

The idea of making a long-distance relationship work for the six months I'd be in a totally different country seemed like a stretch. But Scott and I were in love, and he insisted we could make it work. We were three years in. We'd discussed marriage. He knew my dream proposal plan. It simply had to work.

Flash forward five months. I had just a month left in my beautiful German town nestled in the Black Forest, and I was desperately homesick. I was talking to Scott over Skype — though he refused to chat via video — and he uttered the dreaded words of universal understanding: "I need to take a break." I don't remember specifics after that. Just hot tears, fierce denial, and the same question over and over again: "Is there someone else?" He insisted there was no one, but three agonizing weeks later, I discovered he was already with someone else and had probably been with her all along. I found out on Facebook, when they declared to the world that they were in a relationship while I was thousands of miles away, still thinking I was in a relationship.

Coldplay's fourth album, *Viva la Vida or Death and All His Friends,* was released about a month before my breakup. It's an album brimming with electronic flourishes that burst in your ears like fireworks but then melt into raindrops. It's also an album with all kinds of love-lust and scorned love and sweet love and forbidden love painted into the songs, so it was both difficult and essential listening right after my breakup.

The most important song for me on the album — the one that made it through to the other side of the experience — was "Lovers in Japan." It's a rhythmically intoxicating song that grabs hold of your entire body and beckons it to move in some way. On forest bike rides, with the backdrop of gorgeous, larger-than-life green mountains and a babbling brook keeping me company, this song gave me hope. It made me feel like everything was going to be okay — like I was going to be okay.

I'm back in my car, and my heart is swelling with this feeling again. There is just a touch of loss — not of the boy, because boys come and go. Instead, it's the loss of the self that I was when this particular boy knew me, because that girl is gone. More than any of that though, it is the swell of pride. A sheltered girl from suburban Texas got on a plane by herself and traveled all over the German countryside, alone with her thoughts. The driving piano reminds me of all of the experiences I got to have, just to myself. The insistent but gentle drums are the turning of a page, opening onto a huge new chapter in my life.

I grew up so much in that world. I felt real, heartbreaking loss for the first time — and I survived it. I still marvel at that girl who hopped onto trains by herself to visit Cologne, London, and Berlin, who rode a bike to a street festival and spent time with people who spoke a different language. If you looked at the sheet music of the song, you could see the round, black notes of the song swollen with these little victories.

Suddenly, I'm awake, I'm alive, and the road ahead is full of possibilities.

26 "Careless Memories"
DURAN DURAN

By **Laurie Jakobsen**

It was Easter break 1983. I was going over to my friend Diane's house — this was when cable TV was still a novelty, and her house was wired. Diane wanted me to see Duran Duran when they performed on the Nickelodeon show "Off the Record."

I had met Diane in fifth grade, and she was the one who had always introduced me to new music. She got me into the Doors, then Adam Ant, and I remember her showing me the Soft Cell 12-inch single for "Tainted Love" — my first exposure to the extended dance remix. I found the music entertaining, but not particularly relatable.

In April of '83, I was mid-way through seventh grade, my first year in junior high. It had not been a good year. On top of all the usual adolescent, transitional issues of a suburban teenage girl, tragedy had struck my family hard the previous November. My mother's youngest sister, the one everyone said I took after, had killed herself right before Thanksgiving. To say I was still shell-shocked is an understatement.

Duran Duran's "Off the Record" performance had been taped in late 1981, well before the Nickelodeon airing. Their second album

Rio had not been recorded yet; the iconic videos in exotic locales were still in the future. I remember being intrigued with the first few songs, but not terribly impressed. The show's material was taken mainly from the first album. It kicked off with "Friends of Mine," heavy on the dry ice — or perhaps the footage was just fuzzy; in reviewing it again, I can't say it was much clearer when I sat on Diane's den rug, two feet from the screen.

"Faster than Light" I found interesting as lead singer Simon LeBon started to get into the part. His awareness of the camera increased, and the ham factor went up. "Girls on Film" — I recognized that one. The crowd started to come alive, and Simon's characteristic windmill dancing became more aerobic. Then, "Careless Memories" began.

The beginning was almost obscured; on the album, it started with the drum tick, and then the repetitive keyboard riff — like the click of being on the highway, or in a train — or pacing back and forth. Simon's performance was frenetic; he rushed to the microphone to spit out: "*So soon just after you've gone / My senses sharpen / But it always takes so damn long / Before I feel how much my eyes have darkened.*"

He had my full attention. My chest tightened as I heard those lines.

Watching Duran Duran just a few months after my aunt's death, I was frozen as I absorbed each line. This was the song that expressed how I felt about her loss. It was about the proximity of my grief, the simultaneous experience of rage, dulling depression, and confusion.

Then, the chorus: "*So easy to disturb, with a thought, with a whisper / With a careless memory, with a careless memory.*"

If you've lost someone, you've likely had this experience — you think you've put your feelings behind you, but then something triggers a memory, and you're shattered again.

Second verse; the guitars ripped in, breaking the obsessive pacing of the percussion and the keyboards. Bridge; various solos — and then the crash when all the parts came back in together and Simon hit the third verse. It concluded with: *"Where are you now? / 'Cause I don't want to meet you / I think I'd die / I think I'd laugh at you / I know I'd cry / What am I supposed to do, follow you?*

And then he erupted: *"Outside the thoughts come flooding back now / I'M JUST TRYIN' TO FORGET YOU!"*

Now, I'm sure Simon LeBon was writing about something else — perhaps a now-trivial college relationship. In the context of my aunt's suicide, it was a much darker thing. This was not her first attempt; my family had tried everything to convince her to live. I saw my mother, my grandfather, my aunt, and my cousins all crumble. Until she died, everyone had told me how alike we were. So where does that leave a scared 13-year-old girl? Was this to be my fate at 29?

It was the first time music had the magic of expressing for me what I could not put into words myself. I wasn't alone in my pain anymore. This gave me the hope that I would make it.

When I went to my first concert to see Duran Duran play at Madison Square Garden almost exactly a year later, I heard them play that song to close their set. Then they came back and played "Rio." I learned that after pain, you can dance. You can be happy, too.

I've seen Duran Duran play countless times since then. When I saw the reunion of the original five members in 2003 at Webster Hall in New York City, "Careless Memories" (and then "Rio") closed out the set. Hearing it again, with Andy Taylor's intense guitar and Roger

Taylor's inimitable tom-tom solo in the middle, I was filled with joy at a perfect sonic memory, my personal reunion with my favorite band. I've now made it well past my 29th birthday; I celebrated my most recent one by seeing them play in Reno. Simon's stage patter included a bit about how the music brings us together — we're never alone. I danced and sang every word.

27

"Roll the Credits"

PETER BJORN AND JOHN

By **Jackie Yaeger**

Peter Bjorn and John are one of those bands that *everyone* tells you to listen to. The first time I did, it happened by accident.

I was working in a mall during my first year of college. For some reason, every time I got stuck on denim duty, "Young Folks" would play and I'd find myself air-whistling.

Years later, I met someone, the kind of "someone" you meet when you immediately go to the bathroom to call your best friend and tell her. Never in my life had I felt so magnetically connected to another human being, like I physically couldn't resist being pulled from him.

We couldn't stop kissing while first getting to know each other. We waited in line to get croissants from my favorite bakery, then kissed on my couch for hours — the taste of buttery pastry and warm chocolate still lingering on our tongues.

He didn't live anywhere near me, so each time we saw each other, we had absolutely no clue how long it would be until the next time. He was headed to New York, two hours from my then apartment in Philadelphia. Like "they" always tell you never to do, I followed him there. That night, we kissed while playing cards, and we kissed between sharing what I had in my record collection and who had just broken his heart.

I don't know how much time passed before I realized that music was playing.

I'm not sure if it was the track's drumroll-esque vibrating strings, or the lyrics that broke me from the spell of this guy's eyes, lips, and teeth, but in an instant, we were looking at each other instead of kissing and I was hearing "Roll the Credits" for the first time. The lines that hit me talked about taking the easy way out, running away for good, and bringing the curtains down.

This is exactly what I was feeling about this person, with whom I had a completely unforeseeable future, yet who I could picture walking with me barefoot in the backyard.

None of this existed until after "Roll the Credits," which, in that moment, influenced a quasi out of body experience — when your soul leaves your bones and watches you take your last breath from above until it floats away into heaven, or hell, or space.

Was everyone right? Was Peter Bjorn and John the greatest band of all time? Did it mean that I should pull the curtains down and leave, run anywhere with this person?

These are the questions I ask myself now, whenever I hear the first few cinematic notes of the song.

From there, I think about then.

Then, while this song was on, I left my own body to speed forward to a fake future. I saw us hop out of the hotel bed, still half-clothed. We'd run outside into the slippery, sparkly wet streets of New York and chase down cabs with our stuff falling out of bags behind us. We'd kiss and kiss and hitch rides, cruise down endless highways with nothing to see but sky. We'd look at each other, laughing, and ask "What are we doing?!" We'd end up barefoot in that backyard, with flowers stuck in my hair, and flowing out of his pants pockets.

Suddenly, I swooshed back to the present, falling into the moment and landing softly on something perfect.

Put on "Roll the Credits" now and you might as well just leave me where I'm standing. I go away and I get lost in a fuzzy feeling of warm light glowing from a hotel room. I'm in love. I have no concern for what eventually will happen between us. I am totally lost inside someone else and I no longer understand the concept of time.

28 "Shine"
DAVID GRAY
By **Brendan O'Connell**

Songs have a unique ability to speak to us in a way that no other artistic medium can. Lyrics, melodies, and even beats can magnify our feelings of love or loss, infatuation or heartbreak, elation or depression. As life moves on songs move with us, transporting us back to different moments and experiences. Feelings come rushing back, and the memory of those feelings come bubbling to the surface. It may not make you fall in love again with a lost love or wish to be a 16-year-old blasting Zeppelin late at night, but hearing songs again — no matter how many years later — brings those memories to the forefront of consciousness.

David Gray's "Shine" is one of those songs for me. I first heard it on a mix CD a college girlfriend made for me during the height of our relationship. Our situation was pretty typical for young adults about to graduate college. We found each other near the end of senior year and started an intense relationship, an unconsciously defensive maneuver against the impending changes that were coming upon graduation. I remember getting the mix CD and relishing the gift and the thought behind it. Kids today can't appreciate the fine art of the mixtape or CD. Each one I made for a girlfriend or girl I wanted to date was finely crafted and painstakingly ordered: nothing too strong in the beginning, with just the right amount of romance and affection. I took this gift of a mix CD as much more than just a collection of songs. To me, it was a testament to her feelings for me and a musical love letter.

I probably skipped over "Shine" the first few times I listened to the CD. There were other love songs in the collection that I enjoyed more, and although I'd heard some David Gray before, I hadn't paid close attention to his lyrics. But as graduation (and the end of our relationship) approached, I intently listened to every track again in search of a hidden meaning in her song selection that hinted at a possible future together. She was wiser than I was and saw the relationship more clearly — merely a fling at the end of college. Gray says as much in the opening lines of the song. Being the hopeless romantic that I was, I willfully ignored the opening stanza and chose to cling to hope offered in a single lyric. If David Gray didn't know what waited in the wings of time, then neither did we!

Her words and the surface meaning of the song did not seem to match up with our reality, however. Predictably, the closer our graduation date got, the more time we spent together and the more intense the relationship became. Even as I drove her to the airport after graduation, we listened to the mix CD together, holding hands and crying our eyes out (what a scene that must have been for airport security to behold). I played the song on repeat as I drove from college back home to Chicago the next day, waiting for that "who knows" lyric toward the end of the first verse. I wore the damn thing out every night that summer, reliving the last few weeks of college and that teary ride to the airport every time.

There was no future for us. I moved to South Korea toward the end of the summer, and she went home to pay off college loans. It was painful to hear "Shine" for a few years since it reminded me of her, but mostly because I came to realize how foolish my hopes — and my reading of the song — had been. Like most lost love, eventually the pain subsided, and I could look back on those days with a clearer mind. When I hear "Shine" these days, I place emphasis on different lyrics and hear the tune with a new perspective. The chorus, sung so intensely by David Gray, resonates deeply. Gray didn't write a song about making a dying relationship last at any cost. His song is about building a life without the person for whom you had such intense feelings. It's about learning to let go of your past love and refusing to let it hinder your future. We can't compromise ourselves or force love that isn't meant to be.

In that sense, "Shine" has a new and deeper meaning in my life. I have found love and built a family and home with someone else. I am pursuing a career in music and love what I do. I have been able to shine.

29

"Reservations"
WILCO

By **Kara Murphy**

Jeff Tweedy's somber voice echoed from the mid-size Sony boom-box. It was nestled on the bottom shelf of the entertainment center in the West Hollywood, California apartment I shared with my boy-friend. The year was 2002, and we had planned on getting married someday in the near future, but everything we had built towards was gradually beginning to unravel. We sat there, listening to Wilco's "Reservations" from the *Yankee Hotel Foxtrot* album. I put the pro-motional copy I had of the CD on, in haste, because the proper words had escaped me when trying to explain the growing chasm between us. I was at a loss for coming up with a coherent way to explain my behavior, as I was the one most at fault.

Tears streamed down both our faces as we sat in silence, hold-ing hands but sitting across from each other at an awkward, almost hostile distance in our dimly-lit living room. "I can't reach you any-more," he would tell me. "It frustrates me how I can never really tell what you're thinking." The possibility of a break up was looming, the antithesis of the happy ending both of us envisioned when we first started dating.

One week prior to our mutual revelation that things were growing increasingly dire, I had attended an industry screening of Wilco's documentary *I Am Trying to Break Your Heart*. The parallels between the dynamics mapped out in the film and those at work in my own reality were unmistakable. The band's future, and the industry in which we were both inextricably entangled, were in flux. Emotions ran high, tempers flared, stress was a constant. It mirrored my own life perfectly. I was uncertain about the career I had chosen right out of college; it wasn't the most stable option, even though I loved it. The struggle to stay afloat both emotionally and financially was real.

I had a wonderful, caring, supportive partner in my life — the type of guy that my closest friends likened to winning the lottery. To them, everything looked idyllic — well, for two people in their early twenties. What they saw of our relationship was little more than a facade, on my end. I had no idea where I was headed, what could make me intrinsically happy, or who I really was. That may sound like a first-world existential crisis caused by my being focused entirely on self-actualization, but there was nothing that could possibly console me. There were so many unanswered questions, too many unknown variables. I couldn't be the person he needed, and I let us both down in the end.

The quote, "Anything that is too stupid to be spoken is sung," is attributed to Voltaire. It still gets tossed around in conversations about music centuries after it was first uttered. Yet when I was at a loss for words, the only thing I could think of was to play "Reservations" from *Yankee Hotel Foxtrot*, the accompanying soundtrack from the documentary I had just seen.

Simple in execution, yet utterly gut-wrenching in its progressing depths, it clearly communicated how I felt. I loved this person for whom I was playing the song, but I just couldn't be enough for him with every other internal battle I was waging. As the song ended, he smiled through his tears and nodded in understanding. We made eye contact for the first time in an hour and, ultimately, remained together a while longer. The song had bought us a little more time.

I've attended hundreds of concerts since that fateful evening, embarked on countless road trips with friends, ex-lovers, and acquaintances. While many songs carry a special meaning or vivid memory, none have come close to being as powerful as "Reservations." Every time I hear it play, it conjures up that exact moment and transports me back in time. It holds a permanent spot among my most loved songs, but not for the reason one might expect.

I would move up to the Bay Area six months later, on my own. There was a heaviness I carried in my heart, but it gradually faded. I realized, over time, that we were perhaps ill-suited for each other in the long run. "Reservations" holds a new place in my heart when I listen to it now. This is because I've grown to love, know, and accept myself over time.

The song, and the person for whom I played it, are magnificent gifts bequeathed to me by the universe. I'm reminded of what it's like to be cared for, and I've avoided many would-be "suitors" with ill intentions because I'm able to easily recognize what a genuine love looks like from the very beginning. The experience of "Reservations," in the end, has made me believe that regardless of what happens in my life, I will always be more than enough — for the right person.

30

"Baby When The Light"
DAVID GUETTA

By **Bas Grasmayer**

I pulled her closer to me as the taxi drove down the long road to the airport. We had met two months earlier. I wasn't supposed to fall in love. When arriving at Sofia, Bulgaria, on a five-month work placement, I had told myself that if I was going to fall in love, it had to be in the first two months. I had broken my rule and it was too late. Perhaps it was destined to be broken.

Now, with this midnight taxi to the airport, I was leaving not just a country, but also a place in time. We hugged as the taxi drove us to our final destination. I didn't really know if I would ever see her again; I had not yet made up my mind. I never asked what she was thinking in that moment. We were silent, wrapped in thick winter clothes, and focused on the sensation of each other's touch, a sensation we weren't sure we would experience again.

Our silence was complemented by late night radio programming. In Eastern Europe, more often than not, this means loud, catchy dance music. "Baby When The Light" roared from the speakers.

It was a David Guetta song, which had been receiving a lot of airplay in previous months. It sought to worm its way into my mind, but I tried to resist. I was determined to not let some cheesy pop track become part of this memory. Yet it was the perfect soundtrack for the moment.

The song had been out for about the same length of time that we had known each other. I had been spending a lot of time with a new friend, a professional pop producer, who owned a studio near my house. This opened me up to this type of music. This was a love song, and the lights were very much going out. Outside, Sofia lay covered in darkness. The only things that remained in focus were the two of us and the road ahead, which was rapidly disappearing under the taxi, and the music.

The lyrics about affection and the unknown wormed their way into my mind. I relented and let the song seize the moment, seize the memory.

I don't recall much else from that day, other than taking out a half year's worth of empty beer bottles from the balcony of the apartment I had been renting. Those bottles represented six incredible months in the life of a student who had suddenly found himself in a country where his money could get him three or four times as much alcohol, or anything else, as it could back home.

I do not remember packing. I do not remember closing the door behind me for the last time. I do not remember getting into the taxi. I do not remember our goodbye at the airport. All I remember is that moment.

We did meet again. And again, and again, spending many happy years together since. We have lived together in three different countries, including Bulgaria, where I ended up spending another year. Never did this song become "our song." I couldn't let it. I never even told her about this song. This was always my moment, my memory of us, and a humbling lesson that sometimes you don't get to choose the music — but it chooses you.

ACKNOWLEDGEMENTS

Thank you to everyone who contributed an essay to this collection. I loved reading and editing your words, and most importantly, I enjoyed hearing and sharing your stories. This project wouldn't be possible without the time you invested in your essays. I also want to thank everyone who submitted a story pitch for consideration, but didn't have free time to finish writing one. I still appreciate the ideas that you shared. I also want to thank everyone who listened to me talk about this book and encouraged me to get started.

I want to thank my best friend and podcast co-host Cortney Harding for helping me to edit this book. I wouldn't have been able to finish it without your help and guidance. Thank you for the hundreds of hours of Skype chats and thousands of email exchanges that we've had in the past few years. We are both broken people who wish for a brand new music app every day, but forget about the ones that came out last month.

I also want to thank my mentor Bruce Houghton. You're like a father and friend wrapped into one person. You have played a significant role in my life and career. You always believed in my ability to chase dreams. I still don't know how you found my essay on an obscure blog eight years ago, but I'm happy that you did and thankful that you published my writing. Who would've imagined that you'd find *Hypebot*'s first paid writer and long-time evangelist in a farm boy from North Dakota? I think neither one of us would have believed it if someone told us how much our lives would be shaped by a Google Alert, which is still my best guess for how you found my essay.

I also owe a significant debt of gratitude to Eric Garland, who provided me with mentorship and friendship throughout my time in Los Angeles. You helped me navigate the journey of my life and find my place at Live Nation Labs. You helped me through the most chaotic period of my twenties. I'll never forget the time that you took me across the street for ramen noodles for lunch. You dropped what you were doing and took care of me. I'll also never forget the entire Secret Tacos adventure and the fun times we had.

And, of course, dear reader, thank you for buying and reading this book.

MEET THE CONTRIBUTORS

Matthew Billy has worked in broadcasting since 2003, first at 90.7 WFUV with iconic on-air personalities Vin Scelsa and Pete Fornatale, and then at Sirius XM Satellite Radio. He is also an accomplished record producer, having helmed projects for Pete Seeger, Aztec Two-Step, and Richard Barone. His Between the Liner Notes podcast series fuses his passion for great stories with a lifelong obsession with music and the people that make it.

Michael Cerda has a 20-year background in building products and services in music, video, social, and communications. Cerda spent three years leading the product team at Vevo, building its owned and operated properties and apps and expanding them internationally. Prior to Vevo, Cerda led product development at Myspace on Artists, Events, and Communications. Cerda founded and ultimately sold group messaging startup Threadbox to Myspace, after founding communications companies Ooma and Jangl. Cerda is also the musical director for Latin Jazz ensemble El Desayuno, and lives with his family in the San Francisco Bay Area.

Sam Chennault has shared tequila with Nas, bummed a smoke from El-P, and been scolded by Chuck D. He once saw P. Diddy land on a beach in Miami while wearing a jetpack. In between these major life accomplishments, he's worked as the merchandising lead for Google Play Music, the managing editor for Rhapsody, and the music editor for Miami New Times. He's currently living in San Francisco, engaged, and heading up the content marketing firm, Third Bridge Creative.

Jay Coyle is the founder and "Music Geek" at the digital marketing firm, Music Geek Services. His company provides artist services for the music industry. He is currently working with Sloan, Letters To Cleo, Blake Babies, and The Figgs. Jay's core focus is to help further the careers of artists while partnering with them in a "D.I.Y. +" sort of way to make sure they have long-lasting and fan-focused careers.

Joey Flores is an entrepreneur and musician from Los Angeles, California. He writes political and social spoken word, as well as highly opinionated music industry commentary.

Julian Gijsen is the co-founder and CEO of kollekt.fm, a growing community of curators who select the best music every day — for themselves as well as for brands they are connected to.

Bas Grasmayer is a Dutch serial expat who has previously lived in Bulgaria, Istanbul, and Moscow. He works as a music startup consultant, and is the former product lead of Zvooq, the leading music streaming service in Russia and CIS.

Katie Liestman is an artist manager and marketing strategist who lives in Dallas, Texas. Her previous music ventures include My New

Release and Magnolia Red, which helped artists manage all aspects of their businesses.

Cortney Harding is a startup consultant and writer based in Brooklyn, New York. She is the author of *How We Listen Now: Essays and Conversations about Music and Technology*, blogs weekly for *Cuepoint*, and co-hosts the Music Biz Podcast.

Shelly Hartman is a music industry executive who has specialized in digital marketing, sales, and technology for over 15 years. Shelly has created marketing campaigns for such storied record labels as Priority Records, Capitol, and Universal in addition to managing the digital music presence and artist relations for Sony and T-Mobile.

Darren Hemmings founded Motive Unknown, a strategic digital marketing agency, in September 2011. The company's first client was Infectious Music and the first campaign was Alt-J's platinum-selling "An Awesome Wave." Since then, clients have included Sony RED, Domino Records, Brownswood, BMG Rights Management, Fabric, PIAS, and more, across campaigns for the likes of Smashing Pumpkins, Moby, Faith No More, Jack Savoretti, Superdiscount, Drenge, and Villagers. In addition to artist campaigns, the company also handles all partnerships and marketing for the AIM Independent Music Awards and teaches digital marketing practice for Generator, AIM, and IMRO, among others.

Tony Hymes is an entrepreneur, writer, and international citizen. He is currently pursuing his MBA while working as a Digital Analyst at Disney. Obsessed with music, he helped to build Whyd, a social platform for music lovers. He speaks four languages and lives in Paris.

Laurie Jakobsen is the founder of Jaybird Communications, a PR firm specializing in digital businesses, especially startups, B2B, and music-related ventures. She lives in New York City with her husband Mac Randall and daughter, and has seen a lot of Duran Duran concerts since 1984.

Dane Johnson is a poet and lyricist who rambles all over the world, writing and exploring. When he's not traveling, he retreats to the foothills of Northern California to run up and down canyons and dive into cold rivers. His website: www.ramblewithaplan.com.

Mike King is a course author, instructor, and the Assistant Vice President for Marketing and Recruitment/Chief Marketing Officer at Berklee Online, the online continuing education division of Berklee College of Music. Prior to working at Berklee, Mike was the Marketing/Product Manager at Rykodisc, where he oversaw marketing efforts for label artists including Mickey Hart, Jeb Loy Nichols, Morphine, Jess Klein, Voices On The Verge, Bill Hicks, The Slip, Pork Tornado (Phish), and Kelly Joe Phelps, as well as Frank Zappa's estate. Mike was the Director of Marketing and Managing Editor of Herb Alpert's online musician's resource, www.artistshousemusic.org, for three years.

Sachi Kobayashi is an amateur transcendentalist and part-time culture vulture who has worked in the music industry for over a decade. She has her master's in Communication Management from USC Annenberg, where her research focused on American ethnomusicology, digital media, and public radio.

Alex May is a musician and audio engineer based in Atlanta, Georgia. Having a keen interest in music technology and how it affects artists and listeners, he's penned pieces for *Hypebot*, and worked on the Music Biz Podcast. He hopes to move to the United Kingdom in the not-so-distant future, and pursue music performance and recording in the country that produces his favorite media.

Alison McCarthy is a writer at *eMarketer*, where she spends her days thinking about how different groups of people use the Internet. She has been a contributor to a variety of online publications covering topics in digital media and technology, including *PSFK*, *Hypebot*, and *gnovis*, Georgetown University's journal of communication, culture, and technology. She has a BA in Media Studies from Emerson College and an MA in Media, Culture, and Communication from New York University.

Kara Murphy is a freelance marketing consultant with over 15 years of experience working for major brands in both music and technology, including Rdio, BitTorrent, Premiere Radio Networks, Warner Bros. Records, SF MusicTech, and Pearson Education. She writes for local Bay Area music and culture blog *Spinning Platters* and, as an avid live music photographer, works on the in-house teams for the likes of Outside Lands Music Festival and Noise Pop.

Brendan O'Connell is a musician based in Chicago. He is the songwriter and keyboardist for pop/soul band The Right Now and produces his own music as Sidepart. Follow him on twitter at @ therightnow.

Jackie Otero is a music business educator and consultant in Orlando, Florida. She began her career promoting artists in San Francisco in 2001 and has since worked with Ian Axel of A Great Big World, Clap Your Hands Say Yeah, Aimee Mann, Marc Cohn, Stroke 9, and Speech of Arrested Development, among others. In 2006, she co-founded artist management and music licensing company Front Burner Music in Brooklyn, New York. She has authored a music licensing-focused "Industry Insider" column for alternative music publication *The Comet,* and produced artist showcases at festivals such as CMJ Music Marathon (New York) and Mission Creek Music Festival (San Francisco). She currently serves as the program director of the Entertainment Business and Music Business bachelor's degree programs at Full Sail University.

Derek Pinnick is a lifelong North Dakotan, first from Minot, and then Fargo. He's been playing in bands and going to basement shows pert' near 15 years now, he reckons. He currently plays bass in a Fargo band called Boxcutter Kids, which you can hear on Spotify, Rhapsody, BandCamp, and other places.

Thomas Quillfeldt is a London-based writer and researcher who darts back and forth between PR and journalism. With a background in music and the music business, he also writes and manages projects about video games, technology, marketing, and ecommerce. If Twitter hasn't imploded at the time of your reading this, he can likely be found tweeting complete nonsense at @tquillfeldt.

Marc Ruxin is the former COO and CMO of Rdio, where he oversaw marketing, business development, programming, and advertising. He joined Rdio through their acquisition of TastemakerX, the leading social music platform he founded and ran between 2011 and 2014. Marc has a BA from Hamilton College and an MBA from Columbia Business School, and lives in San Francisco with his wife and three children. Marc blogs about music and film at www.snoozebutton.com and the *Huffington Post.*

Caitlin Teibloom loves pop, hip-hop, and rock 'n' roll. She writes about this love all over the Internet from her home in Austin, Texas, which she shares with her wonderful husband and nutball dog, Scooby.

Amanda Krieg Thomas is a music supervisor for film and TV. She is currently at Neophonic, working on TV shows such as "American Horror Story," "Scream Queens," and "American Crime Story." Past projects include "Fake Off" (truTV), "Grace Stirs Up Success" (American Girl/Mattel), and "French Dirty" (Homegrown Pictures). She occasionally dispenses industry advice and music recommendations on www.tadpoleaudio.com.

Emily White is the co-founder of the New York and Los Angeles management and consulting firm Whitesmith Entertainment. Through White's varied background in the music industry, Whitesmith's approach in their work with musicians, comedians, and athletes has always been to take the artists' perspective while simultaneously taking care of the fans. White additionally serves on CASH Music's Board and The Grammys Education Committee in New York, while working with artists such as Matthew Friedberger and Fox Stevenson. In 2012, White began managing Olympic gold medalist Anthony Ervin due to her strong personal background in competitive swimming. Managing Anthony like the rock star he is led to a crowdfunding campaign, as White manages athletes in the same she works with musicians. Realizing that there was no vertical in the crowdfunding space that specifically serviced sports properly, White co-founded Dreamfuel recently with Justin Kalifowitz, bringing her modern music work to the sports industry and beyond.

Solveig Whittle is a musician, music marketer, and blogger who regularly contributes articles to indie and DIY music industry websites, blogs, and podcasts. She teaches social media to music students at the Art Institute of Seattle, and is an instructor at the University of Washington in their Professional and Continuing Education certificate program for social media. Solveig is an alt-pop vocalist and lyricist (BMI) who has released four DIY albums. She is a voting member of the Pacific Northwest Chapter of NARAS (The Grammys˙).

Jackie Yaeger is a Brooklyn-based twenty-something, obsessed with magazines, eavesdropping, Instagram, lipstick, and living every night like it's Friday. Her first-ever live music experience was seeing the Backstreet Boys' "Backstreet's Back Tour" in 1998 in Philadelphia, where she donned snap-on pants and pigtail buns. Somewhere between a "Band-Aid" and "The Enemy," Jackie interviews bands about where they've tasted the best pizza in the world, ghostwrites their bios, and concepts cool editorial features to help promote their tours.

ABOUT THE EDITOR

Kyle Bylin is a user researcher and trade journalist who specializes in music streaming services and consumer behavior trends. He is the author of *Promised Land: Youth Culture, Disruptive Startups, and the Social Music Revolution*, a collection of essays that chronicles how disruptive startups and digital youth reshaped the music industry and created a musical utopia for today's listeners.

He has conducted user research and developed consumer insights for two music technology companies, SoundHound Inc. and Live Nation Labs. He authored internal reports on why people attend live concerts and how they listen to and discover music in their daily lives, among many other topics. He has also served as a chart manager at *Billboard* magazine and as blog editor at *Hypebot.com*.

Bylin co-hosted and produced *Hypebot*'s Music Biz Podcast, an audio program which provided its listeners with in-depth commentary and interviews featuring music industry executives. He has been featured as a source in news stories by *The New York Times*, *Rolling Stone*, *The Fader*, *NPR*, *Marketplace Money*, and *MTV News*.

He currently lives and works in Fargo, North Dakota.

PERMISSIONS

Careless Memories

Words and Music by Andy Taylor, John Taylor, Nick Rhodes, Roger Taylor and Simon Le Bon

Copyright (c) 1981 Gloucester Place Music Ltd.

All Rights Administered by Sony/ATV Music Publishing LLC, 424 Church Street, Suite 1200, Nashville, TN 37219

International Copyright Secured All Rights Reserved

Reprinted by Permission of Hal Leonard Corporation

The Luckiest

Words and Music by Ben Folds

Copyright (c) 2001 Free From The Man Songs LLC

All Rights Administered by BMG Rights Management (US) LLC

SHARE YOUR SONG STORY

Do you have a song that has shaped your identity and changed your life? Do you have a song that has become tied to a story of your life? Would you like to share your song story in the next volume of this book? If you would like to share your song story with us for future consideration, please send us a message at songstoriesproject@gmail.com.

For a playlist of the songs referenced in
***Song Stories*, visit www.songstories.org.**